Whispers in the Walls

New Black and Asian Voices from Birmingham

Edited by
Leone Ross and Yvonne Brissett

TINDAL STREET PRESS

First published in 2001 by
Tindal Street Press Ltd,
217, The Custard Factory, Gibb Street, Birmingham B9 4AA
www.tindalstreet.org.uk

Commissioning Editor: Jackie Gay
Copy Editor: Emma Hargrave
Typesetting: Tindal Street Press Ltd

Leone Ross's 'Covenant' first appeared in *Obsidian III: Literature in the
African Diaspora* (North Carolina State University, 2001).

A CIP catalogue reference for this book is
available from the British Library.

ISBN 0 9535895 5 2

Printed and bound in Great Britain by
Biddles Ltd, Woodbridge Park Estate, Guildford.

Acknowledgements

Leone Ross
I would like to thank those who always support me in this path: Carol, Soroya, Bobby and Jenne. And Yvonne, for her unwavering patience and clear vision at two o'clock in the morning.

Yvonne Brissett
For their inspiration, love and support, I would like to thank my family and friends; in particular, my parents, Elaine, Carl, Linda and Donna. And Leone, for sharing her knowledge and experience.

We would both like to thank Tindal Street Press for giving us the opportunity to edit this collection, and in particular Jackie Gay and Emma Hargrave for their encouragement and sensitivity. Thank you to all the workshop facilitators, Roi Kwabena, Jackie Gay, Polly Wright, Ranjit Khutan, and especially Martin Glynn for his commitment to the word.

Contents

Introduction

Whispers are weapons. Anyone who has ever been the target of gossip knows the discomfort of winks, snide remarks behind hands, the feeling of being watched and discussed. When black and Asian people first began arriving in the UK in serious numbers we were often seen as outsiders, we were whispered about and had to hold up our heads in the face of curiosity, ignorance and prejudice.

Whispers are powerful and cannot be stopped; anyone who has ever belonged to a disenfranchised group knows this. Throughout history people who had no voice have used drum beats, songs, stories and folklore to communicate with one another under threat of violence, unjust law, fear of extermination. Whispers can tell of impending rebellion, get help to someone who needs it, share joy and sorrow. We all engage with our whispered inner voice as we grow as individuals: make mistakes, feel fear, celebrate victory.

It is no surprise, then, that whispers are often used as a narrative tool in literature: characters whisper truths to themselves at moments of stress and reflection and revelation. The stories in this multifaceted collection are by mainly unpublished black and Asian writers from Birmingham –

they tell of all these kinds of whisper: their complex nature; the effects of years of mutterings; the ways one deals with them, for better or worse.

The whispers are everywhere; so are the walls, the urban and domestic geography. The Bull Ring, Handsworth Park, the Coventry Road – these places hold distinct experiences and memories for 'minority' communities and they reappear from many different perspectives in the stories: the city itself is a motif, the tales are unflinching. A woman returns to her childhood home to exorcise the ghosts of her past, another rises above the nosy whispers of the Soho Road. One man has a passion for the reggae dance hall; another is fascinated by the history in his grandfather's feet. A man in distress leaves his tower block to move through the shadows of the night-time city; a son longs simply to communicate with his father; a woman returns defiantly to her church; a pregnant girl flees judgement and pain – these are stories that challenge, touch, delight and enthral. Women murder men in this book. People go mad in this book. They also fall in love, nurture their children against great odds, explain complex cultural patterns and explore their own emotional and physical landscapes.

Whispers in the Walls grew out of a series of writing workshops held at community venues across Birmingham in collaboration with the Millennibrum Project. We worked with raw, unheard voices, bringing to the surface a wealth of creative talent. When invited to edit this anthology, we were proud to work closely with these writers. They come from all over the city and use dialect, letters and verse as well as prose to tell their stories. We anticipate that this groundbreaking work will help launch the careers of more Birmingham writers, following the success of *Hard Shoulder* in 1999.

More than anything, this anthology tells – in defiance,

revelation and humour – of our constant *presence*. The stories, experiences and emotions of black and Asian people are soaked into the walls of this city. We have been here for centuries, and although we have not always been seen, acknowledged or recognized, we have always told each other stories: to comfort, explain, to hear the sounds of our own voices. *Whispers in the Walls* puts those voices up on the stage and projects them across and beyond the city.

Right now, it's an exciting time for Birmingham. The heart of the UK is under reconstruction. In March 2001, Birmingham City Council published a report on race equality in Birmingham – *Challenges for the Future* – which pinpoints diversity as a key feature of this vibrant, modern city, and encourages its citizens to regard this as a major asset. The study also highlights the rapidly changing demography of the area. The indications are that 'minority ethnic communities will form a majority of the population over the next two decades'. We are the future. Our whispers have become louder as we move into mainstream society and assert our identities. We are here; in the walls, in schools and churches, in nightclubs, the workplace, whispering our tales. All with the streets and vibe and sound of Birmingham, ever present, ever sure.

Leone Ross and Yvonne Brissett
April 2001

Letters A Yard

Maeve Clarke

April 1960

Dear Mamma,

Hope that this letter reach you as it leave me, in good health. Well, we reach England safe and sound. Ship journey long and did make me feel sick. Me glad me feet finally on firm ground. The streets of Birmingham not pave with gold like them tell you back home and the city ugly. Them have a place call the Bull Ring but me don't see no bull yet. Nico find a house. We have to share with some Indian people but we have two rooms of our own. Lucky Nico is a trained accountant, otherwise him wouldn't find job so quick. If him work hard there is a good chance of promotion. I hope to find a job soon, with my nurse training it shouldn't be too difficult. If everything go all right we will be able to come home in the five years like we plan and build the house of our dreams. Kiss Laura for me. Tell her Mummy and Daddy miss her, and as soon as we settle we will send for her. In the meantime I send you a little something for her keep.

I am your daughter,

Munchie

'Bus conductor? How you mean bus conductor?'

'Dem seh me qualifications nuh recognize here. But if I show my worth, by the time I retrain and get me English qualifications there will be a job fi me.'

'At least you have a job and we have a little money. Nuh bother worry, Nico. Your time will come.'

July 1960

Dear Mamma,

How keeping? Sunshine come, not very strong but it better than nothing. Seem like it rain every day since we reach the mother country. Them crying out for nurses in England, so me soon find job. Once we build our house we can all live together. Kiss Laura for me. Hard to think she two next month. You wouldn't believe how I miss her. We send some money for her birthday. Hope it arrive safe.

I am your daughter,
Munchie

'Why you love waste money so? You nuh see all the bills we have fi pay?'

'But I couldn't let me first-born birthday pass without sending something.'

'De pickney two years old. She nuh even know what day call, much less seh is her birthday. Cho!'

December 1960

Dear Mamma,

Hope this reach you as it leave me, in good health. Christmas soon come. Praise the Lord! It winter here now and snow fall everywhere. Look like summer blossom when it drop – it so pretty and white. Mr Singh from the house say we lucky, this year winter not too bad – but the cold still lick me bones. Luckily, we have gas fire so me don't stay cold for long. Me have an interview at St Chad's Hospital after Christmas. Here's hoping that the New Year bring good things for all of us. Me send a little something for you and Laura for Christmas. Hope it reach safe.

I am your daughter,
Munchie

'How it so cold in here?'
'Money done.'
'You nuh have nothing in you purse?'
'No.'
'You mean seh we nuh even have shilling fi put in the meter?'
'No.'
'Cho! England is a bitch!'

February 1961

Dear Mamma,

Still cold here. The snow not so pretty now it turn into dirty slush. I slip and twist me ankle the other day. First time I see me neighbours laugh. Couple of them help me up and talk to me. Them have a funny accent – couldn't understand a word them say – but maybe now me break the ice we can be friends. I get a job in the hospital, not the one I did want because Jamaican training not the same as English training. I tell them sick people is sick people no matter where them stay. But them don't listen. So many people go for this nursing auxiliary job – I lucky to get it. I think is a sign that this year going to be a good one.

I send you a little something for the time being. Soon as me wage start come regular I will send you a little more. Hug me baby for me.

I am your daughter,
Munchie

'You is a nurse. How come them give you this job, a wipe shit?'

'Them seh I have to retrain before I can work as a nurse but at least this way I get work experience in an English hospital.'

'I don't want my woman wipe white man batty.'

'Nuh mind. Soon as we settle I will start my nurse's training.'

'Cho! Bout you a clean shit.'

August 1962

Dear Mamma,

We find a good Baptist church. We go to the morning and evening service on a Sunday, because two of them service make one of ours back home. English people sing low, not like we, and every hymn them sing sound sad. The baptism pool look just like a little swimming pool. Me laugh first time I see Reverend Templar, with him black wellington boots under him white gown ready to do baptism. Him don't preach like pastor back home, him speak very quiet, like him a talk secret, but then, English people more reserved. I suppose it don't matter – there is only one God and the message is the same. What shock me is that nobody dress up for church. Me sure God not too please when him see people worship him in them yard clothes. I dream of Laura every night. Kiss her for me and don't make her forget we.

I am your daughter,

Munchie

'Good evening, Mr and Mrs Samuels. Back again – we can't keep you away, can we?'

'Well, we think that a double helping of God start the week right.'

'You certainly feel the Spirit. I can hear you singing from the pulpit.'

'Yes, Reverend. We feel that as God so high up in heaven we must raise our voices so that he can hear us.'

'I think we all heard you today, including God.'

16

May 1963

Dear Mamma,

Here's hoping this reach you as it leave me, in good health. Beg you tell Laura she soon have a little brother or sister. Baby due November. We getting married next week. In England, people look on you bad if you don't marry before baby come. Nico doing overtime and we looking for a house of our own. I working extra hours too but money still tight so me can't send much. Tell Laura we love her and will send for her soon as we find a house big enough for all of us.

I am your daughter,

Munchie

'You pregnant! How you mean seh you pregnant? How that happen?'

'If you don't know, me can't tell you.'

'But we can't afford baby! We live in two room and we nuh have enough money as it is! How you expect us fi save enough to go back with money in we pocket and build a house? Why you never take more care?'

'Me?'

'Yes, you. This is a woman thing.'

September 1963

Dear Mamma,

The wedding did nice. Only wish you and Laura could come. We marry in Birmingham Register Office – I never want marry in church with me belly a push in front of me. Popsie bake me cake – taste just like one from home. Mr Lee give us some bedspread. Merle make me wedding dress – it short because me never have enough money to buy plenty material. But it white and pretty, just like I always dream. The Singh them make curry, not as good as our curry goat, but it never taste too bad. Nico say him first English pickney must be a boy to carry him name and make him

17

proud. Winter a bite now Christmas coming. I send you a little something and a wedding photo. Show Laura so she don't forget what her mummy and daddy look like. When the baby born I will send you another photograph of the three of us.

I am your daughter,
Munchie

'How you mean seh is gal pickney?'

'Look nuh, is a little girl.'

'But I tell everyone is bwoy we having. You make me look like fool.'

'Not my fault is a girl.'

'No? A who born her? The baby nuh even look like me. Cho man! You cyah even do that right!'

December 1963

Dear Mamma,

We have a little girl. Nico so please him never talk for three days, the emotion make him so happy. After, him buy me a wooden cabinet as a present. It so pretty, Mamma, I can't wait till I have some nice plates and glasses to put in there, but first we must find a house. We don't want to live just anywhere – so we taking our time. Soon as we find somewhere we will send for Laura.

I am your daughter,
Munchie

'You find anything?'

'No. Every time is the same. When dem see me dem seh de house just sell. If I did only come yesterday, or de day before. Bet you next week dem still have "For Sale" sign in the window. It mek me so tired, Munchie. So tired.'

'Hush! We will find something.'

'Is you one keep me strong.'

'If we pull together, we will always be strong. Maybe we can put our name on the council list – get a little place like the Browns them.'

'We not living in no council property. I not begging nobody fi nothing. My money the same colour as everybody else.'

'Yes, but we not.'

'I am a Jamaican. I have my pride.'

August 1965

Dear Mamma,

We still don't find exactly the right house. Every day after work Nico walk all over Handsworth, Bearwood and Smethwick, looking for somewhere for us to live. But it hard. The little gal ah grow. I feel sure you would like her – she quiet and don't give no trouble. But it funny how she feel the cold more than we Jamaican born and bred. We join a pardner draw to help save money for Laura fare. She soon have another brother or sister. Baby due any time now and I going to need help. Hope you get the money I send last time. Can't send so much this time because I stop work now. But I soon make up and send more. I imagine Laura big now. Never mind, she not too big for you to kiss her for me.

I am your daughter,

Munchie

'Is a bwoy!'

'Yes, man! Me first English pickney!'

'How you mean you first English pickney? Wha bout the little gal?'

'Cho man! Gal them nuh count. First man them meet, them run tek him name. This bwoy gwine carry my name all him life. Him even look like me. Me sure him will mek someting of himself, give the English them someting to reckon with. I gwine find us a house if is the last thing I do.'

19

March 1967

Dear Mamma,

Nico find a house in Harborne. We buy it from an Irishman. Him only sell it to us to spite him neighbours, but me don't care. The house lovely. It have three bedrooms, a kitchen, a bathroom and two rooms downstairs. The garden not big like the one back home, but in England seem like everyone want them garden little because them only grow flowers. We have a mortgage now, so we have to wait a little before we send for Laura. We must give thanks to God for the things he provides. God willing we soon come home.

I am your daughter,

Munchie

'We can send fi Laura soon?'

'You nuh see we nuh have no money – we have mortgage and two kids. Better she stay where she deh fi now. Nuh make sense tek her out of school and pay big airfare fi her if we going home soon.'

'But I miss her.'

'I know, but you have two here to occupy you. Nuh cry.'

January 1968

Dear Mamma,

Hope you receive the dresses for Laura and the shoes I send you. Couldn't send the watch like I did promise. Shopkeeper put it to one side for me but when I go back him already sell it. Never mind, next time. Look like we not coming home quite yet – I just have another baby. Him and de first boy favour Nico is a shame. The little gal don't look like nobody but she good. Love her book is a shame. Good thing library free in England. We hope the boy them will turn doctor or lawyer. How is me sweet Laura? Beg you kiss her for me and remind her we soon send for her.

I am your daughter,

Munchie

20

'We soon have another mouth fi feed and you a beg me money fi buy watch!'

'I did promise me mother and I have to lie when I write her.'

'You want to ruin me? Every time you see me start mek someting of meself you beg me fi someting or you come pregnant youself. How you tink seh we ah go feed it? You must tink baby food grow out a yard and nappy hang from tree.'

'I work too, you know. Is my money pay for the food in this house.'

'Oh, you tink seh because you earn a few penny you can talk to me how you please. You better remember that I am the man in this house and if you nuh like it, go find somewhere else live and tek you pickney dem with you.'

September 1968

Dear Mamma,

We get the second boy christen. There are three or four other black families at the church now and them all have small children too. Is good to see that we black people keep up our ways and send the children to church looking nice. English people worship God in them house clothes. The women don't even wear hat, never mind gloves. Every Sunday we black families take turn give dinner. We eat rice and peas and fried chicken. We drink punch, and sing and play record. After dinner the men go in the front room with them rum and play dominoes. It make me feel like me back home. Lord, how I miss it all. We might not have much but we happy with what we have. Blessed are the meek for they shall inherit the earth.

I am your daughter,
Munchie

'Seem like we always de host and never de guest, nuh true?'

'Is one of the few ways we have to mek we feel like we back home.'

21

'True, Nico, but me tired cook fi all dese people that only come with dem empty hand and empty belly.'

'Hush! Me sure people soon start invite us.'

'Me have a good mind fi serve dem all cornmeal porridge next time. Soon see how many ah dem craven Christian come back.'

June 1975

Dear Mamma,

How keeping? Sometimes it seem like only yesterday me leave Jamaica. Nico flying home at the end of this week. Him daddy sick. I don't think it too serious, but as Nico the only child, is him have to go. Beg you tell Laura that her daddy soon come. The money we did save for her fare we have to use pay Nico air ticket. The children growing up now. The little gal studying hard. She have ambition, want make something of herself. I hope she will become a teacher, maybe even a doctor. They are good professions for a woman. The first boy good at maths – but him prefer play football. So long as it don't interfere with him studies, me don't mind. The second boy have sweet tongue and him good with money is a shame. Can sell you down to the very shoes off you feet. Nico bringing Laura school fee money with him. Beg her don't bother fail no more exam and hurry up finish her schooling. I am sending you a few things you can't get over there. The Lord bless you and keep you.

I am your daughter,
Munchie

'Me sorry seh you daddy dead. Him was a good man.'

'Is always the good die first. You know how much it cost me to bury him? Since when Jamaica get so expensive? But everybody see how me send me daddy off in style.'

'So how much money you come back with?'

'You deaf? You nuh hear me seh me haffi show everybody

22

seh me ah bigshot, dat me come from foreign with money in me pocket?'

'You mean seh you spend all ah we little savings? But we nuh have nothing here!'

'Is true. But dem back home don't have to know.'

'And Laura? How she look? How she doing?'

'She never wah talk to me. Seh she nuh have no daddy. Seh her only mother is you mamma. I tell her, children should honour thy father and thy mother, but she suck her teeth on me and seh she nuh know we.'

'Oh Lord! Why you send these things to test me?'

'I did tell you when you start breeding, dat dem pickney would turn round and make you suffer. You sacrifice everything for dem and dem still want more; dem nuh satisfy till dem strip down to the very skin off you back.'

'Why you bring back the steam iron I send Mamma and the sports shoes I send Laura?'

'You mamma already have one. She have television and telephone too. Laura seh she nuh wear sports shoes without name. Is only adidas and Nike she wear, she nuh want people laugh after her.'

'Television and telephone? Adidas and Nike? Something wrong when we who is working so hard nuh have nothing! Wha bout de house? It nearly finish? I want go home.'

'Cho man! Tief steal the tile dem off the roof. Dem even steal down to the toilet seat in the bathroom. All the money I send for materials me tiefin cousin dem use fi dem own property. Something wrong when you own blood steal from you. I find someone else to finish the job – but that mean more money, so we jus gwine haffi work harder. Lucky seh de little gal soon finish school. She can get a job and start pay her way. Bout time after all these years we spend looking after her.'

October 1978

Dear Mamma,

How you mean say Laura pregnant? Who pregnant her? How it happen when she go to private school all her life and she only have one more year before she graduate from college? What she going do now the college throw her out? Say them have them reputation to think bout.

How she going look after the baby? We finally have the money for her fare, but the authorities not going let her in if she come with pickney. We give her the best we could. Everything! More than we give the pickney them in England. How could she do this? How she so ungrateful?

I am your daughter,
Munchie

'What we gwine do bout Laura?'

'You mean what *you* gwine do bout Laura. Is you her mother.'

'We can send fi her now, we have the money.'

'I not paying for no cheeky bitch come live in my house or feed her pickney after the way she treat me in Jamaica.'

'But, Nico, it was only her temper did ah ride her.'

'Look like temper not the only thing ah ride her these days. Mek me grieve when I tink bout all that money I waste on her education. Just better warn the little gal.'

'Bout what?'

'If she pregnant herself, she and the pickney stop out a yard.'

July 1980

Dear Mamma,

A football scout from a big club in London want to sign up the first boy but him daddy won't sign the papers. Say white people only happy when black people chasing after ball and running round track, that way we don't get anywhere in life. The first boy vex but I tell him is for the best – this way him can concentrate on him studies. May God keep you safe until I see you again.

I am your daughter,

Munchie

'It's only the junior team, Dad. I'm still going to do my exams. I'm not stupid, you know. Not everybody can become a top footballer, and even if they do, it's a short stay at the top.'

'You not doing it. Is white man conspiracy to keep us black people down. Look pon the Indian dem. Most of dem come after we, and where dem is now? How many of *dem* you see running up and down grass field?'

'*All right*, Dad. I've heard it all before.'

'Where dem is now? Half ah dem can't even speak English properly, yet dem have shop and restaurant. Dem drive Mercedes and live in big house. Dem son turn architect or lawyer; dem wife respect dem and dem daughter dem nuh come home with dem belly full. And where we black people deh? At the bottom. Jumping up and down in boxing ring, running after ball, or in prison. Black people too stupid. We still think that sport is an opportunity for us. We too fool to know is how dem keep us down.'

'So, you're not signing it then.'

May 1981

Dear Mamma,

Glad to hear Laura marry her baby father and that the college take her back. Hope the money I send to pay her fees reach you. Don't bother mention it to Nico, him don't know about this little Post Office account. The children here think them big and won't listen to them elders. The little gal say she don't want to teach – it boring. She gone to art school, like she think she can live from dropping paint on paper all day. She move to London, say she have more opportunity there. We did want her to stay here but she insist on going. Pity it too far for her to come home and see us. I hope to go visit her soon, if God spare me life.

I am your daughter,

Munchie

'If you go to art school you not living under my roof. I don't want no squatters here.'

'But, Dad . . .'

'Nuh bother "but" me. If you not gwine study to be a teacher or something I can be proud of, go find job and pay you keep. You pickney like beg but you nuh like give.'

'Dad! I want to be an artist.'

'An artist! You must think I born yesterday. All you want is for me to subsidize you so you can spend all day smoking ganja with you nasty little "artist" friends. Well, you can think again.'

'Dad, I want to draw, design things.'

'Liar! You just don't want to work or use you brains.'

June 1985

Dear Mamma,

Sorry me never write you for so long. But you know how it go, what with one thing and another, it difficult find time. The second boy have him final exams soon. Me sure him will do well and make us proud. I must run now, Nico ah call me. Him off work sick. Something to do with him heart, but it not too bad if him take him tablets and don't fret too much. God willing me soon come home.

I am your daughter,

Munchie

'How you mean it nuh matter? You come follow you friends, fail half you exams and you stand there telling me it nuh matter?'

'I don't need exams to start my own business.'

'Business? What business when you cyah even read or write?'

'Course I can, but I don't need a piece of paper to prove it. I'm going to work for myself.'

'Oh yes, with you three-penny stall down the market. Nobody in my family ever work in a market before. You mek me feel shame.'

'I don't want to be like you, Dad – killing myself for a company that doesn't care whether you live or die. Always scrimping and saving. Never having anything. That's not for me. When people look at me I want them to want the clothes I wear, the car I drive and the woman at my side. In five years' time I'll have more money than you've got now.'

'Big word nuh feed hungry cow! When it all go wrong nuh bother come back here! Run go live with you artist sister and her stupid natty dreadlocks friend! Go follow you brother and work in a shop!'

'He's the manager actually, Dad.'

'It not his shop, so it nuh count. With his brains he could have been anything! Anything! Cho! You all make me sick.'

'Well, if you had filled out his grant form he could have become an architect like he wanted.'

'Why should I have to tell the government my business? You all get schooling up till the age of sixteen. You have it easy, not like we back home.'

'Yeah, I know. Up at dawn, feed the pigs, milk the cows, chop wood, walk twenty miles to school –'

'Nuh bother backchat me, bwoy. You pickney have everyting. Never go hungry. Never want for anyting and not one of you doing anyting decent. When me friends talk bout how them children turn surgeon and solicitor I have to keep my mouth shut.'

'Talk about Laura then. Years of private education and

27

she's still trying to finish her degree. She's got two children and a husband and yet you're still giving her money.'

'Dat different! You pickney grow with me and you mother. Laura never have us fi guide her; private school was the only way to make sure she have a good future.'

'If you say so, Dad. If you say so.'

January 1987

Dear Mamma,

Them say the Lord giveth and the Lord taketh away. Him just take the reverend from our church. He died in my hospital but him never recognize me when I visit him. Me sure God will judge him as he deserves. Let us give praise and thanks onto the Lord for He is ever merciful. Shouldn't be too long before I come home to you and me daughter and give her the loving I haven't been able to all these years.

I am your daughter,
Munchie

'Munchie, you see who on de ward?'

'No, Popsie. Who?'

'Mr Templar.'

'Who?'

'Reverend Templar! From church. I forget, you stop going church years back.'

'Wha wrong with him?'

'I don't know and I don't care since I hear two doctors chat bout him.'

'Seh what?'

'Seh him nuh want no black nurse or doctor touch him. Even insist dem write it on him chart.'

'Ah lie. He is a man of God.'

'Nursing Auxiliary Samuels? Fetch a bedpan, quickly please, for Mr Templar. He's at the end of the ward.'

'Yes, Sister.'

'You gwine give that man a bedpan, Munchie?'

'No. I gwine leave it at the foot of the bed where him can see it but cyah reach it. Mek the unrighteous bitch shit himself!'

March 1989

Dear Mamma,

I write you these few lines to let you know I am safe and well. House quiet now the children gone. The little gal still in London – she design book covers. She did always like reading. I don't like her pictures but the company happy, them just give her another contract. The first boy move north and doing well for himself. Him even have him own office – not very big, but is his name on the door. The second boy sell jeans and jumpers and such like. Him plan to open a second-hand shop at the end of the year. I wouldn't buy from there but plenty white people like them bargain, so good luck to him. Nico ready to come home now. Him blood pressure still high and him have gout. Doctor say a warm climate will do him good so long as him take it easy. I will write as soon as I know when we coming.

I am your daughter,

Munchie

'I want to die back a yard.'

'Nuh chat foolishness. You not gwine die. You still young.'

'Me children abandon me and dis is not my country. I don't want to die here. Promise you won't mek me die here.'

15 November 1989

Dear Mamma,

How keeping? Sorry it take me so long to write but you know how it is. We finally sell the house. Nico say is time we go home. I can't wait to see me old friends, see light instead of dark, feel

29

sun instead of rain. I glad the children grow up – I tired and I don't want no more pickney to look after. I work too hard all me life. Is my time come now. We arriving December 15th, in time for Christmas. Can't wait to hug you and me first-born, Laura. This time I going to end the letter like the English do.

Love,
Munchie
xxx

3 December 1989

Dear Munchie,

Sorry to be the bearer of bad news. Laura leave for foreign yesterday. She borrow Maggie daughter (the one that dead in '86 when she come back here on vacation) passport and gone a US to work. Say she want give her children a good start in life. Say she will come back soon as she save a little money. She left the pickney with me but I too old to turn mother again, so them will have to stay with you. Beg you hurry up and come – me don't have no more strength. Hope you have a safe journey and that this letter find you as it leave me, in good health.

I am your same mother,
Mercedes

Matthew 7, Verse 1

Beverley Wood

'To hell with what they're gonna think. They'll just accept you as you are, you'll see.' Joy continued blending coffee-coloured make-up into her skin.

'I've got a bad feeling about this,' Lauren sighed. 'The last time I was there things were different. I was one of them.' She struggled with the sleeve of her blouse. 'They'll just remember me as a backslider, the pregnant slut with no baby to show. "She turn she back on de Lard, and become back-slider"' – she mocked imaginary voices – 'I'll just be another prodigal lamb.'

'Don't be so dramatic. Hey, remember how good the music was? Well, it's even better now – serious rhythm and bass these days,' Joy added.

Arriving early was Lauren's idea. She wanted to sneak in unnoticed and sit in a corner.

The tiny church just off Soho Road still looked impoverished from the outside, even though it had been five years since she'd last visited. Inside, things were different. Someone had bought two huge bouquets of flowers and placed them either side of the faded pulpit, now alive with colour.

That must've taken effort, Lauren thought. *Handsworth's Asian shops certainly don't sell flowers like these.*

As they made their way along the aisle, she might as well have been naked. Heads began to turn. Pure willpower kept her moving, smiling at the astonished faces that examined her. She felt self-conscious.

'Joy, I'm getting a really bad feeling about this. Let's just say we came to see someone and then get out of here.'

'C'mon, chill out. You're feisty enough when you're holding a disability protest banner, just pretend you're doing that, only quietly.'

They sat near the front of the church, the best place for a maximum earful of music. *Joy's right, the music really is good*, Lauren thought. Peering around her she was surprised to see how many faces she remembered. People seemed the same. Except for one thing.

'How come everyone's dressed like they're going to a fashion show? I've never seen so much Gucci in one room!'

Joy kept her head straight ahead and leaned towards her. 'These are the New Age Christians,' she half whispered. 'The minister may have banned jewellery and make-up on his flock, but he didn't mention Gucci, Chanel or Rolex did he? Check out the size of the emerald on Sister Smith's wedding-ring finger.'

'Talk about pushing plainness to its limit!' Lauren laughed, then sneezed, affected by the expensive scents lingering in the air. It was as bad as the perfumery section in Rackhams.

The odd thing was that during the weekdays, most of these people looked very plain, even a bit shabby. But Sundays . . . they were days for ritualistic grooming and dressing up, all in the name of the Lord.

Lauren felt a tap on her shoulder.

'Bless de Lard, my prayers been answered! My eyes not deceiving me, is really you Sista Lauren?' Sister Sylvera's voice was choked with emotion. 'You don't know how many times I've longed to see your lovely face my sister, and here you are today!' She pulled Lauren up into her well-corseted E-cup embrace, and held her tightly.

Stunned, Lauren pulled herself free from the bear hug after a few seconds. She felt annoyed at the invasion, even though the gesture was well-meaning.

'I was so worried when I heard about your accident, but praise God, I can see He gave you the strength to just get on with your life.' Sister Sylvera's eyes skimmed over Lauren's recoiled arm.

So how come you never visited me in all this time? Lauren thought. No one from the church had visited her during the many weeks she'd spent in hospital. She'd been left alone, wondering which parts of her body would still work after the full-on collision with another car. Perhaps it was just as well that they hadn't come, Lauren had reasoned. Their platitudes about Satan, the tests to her faith and how repentance could heal would only have depressed her even more.

'Is it you?' Sister Edmonds stepped up, beaming. She spoke slowly, as always, taking care to keep her Caribbean vowels Anglicized. 'Bless the Lourd, my prayers have been answered! It is so good to see you. I missed you soo much.' She bent forward, stroked Lauren's arm and kissed her cheek. 'Good to see you coping so *pousitively* with the legs and the arms. And you still look as lovely as He created you.'

She always said I look lovely, Lauren thought. There was something palpably irritating about Sister Edmonds. *What she means is she's just glad I'm not wearing make-up or any jewellery. Some things never change.*

But Lauren had changed. Things hadn't been easy for her after the accident. Losing her unborn child in the crash had been devastating enough, but the dread of not knowing how the nerve damage would affect her arms and legs, not knowing whether she would ever walk again or be able to use her arms had been terrifying.

As awkward as she appeared to other people now, she was glad that she could walk and use her arms – albeit with the use of muscle relaxants. Without them, the weak nerve impulses that struggled to connect her spinal cord to her fingertips and toes caused havoc, contracting the wrong muscles at the wrong times.

'You may be disabled,' one of her colleagues in the movement had reassured her, 'but that doesn't mean your life is tragic.'

So Lauren had rebuilt her life her own way and became comfortable and confident about living in her body. But the positive vibes and compassion from the crowd that gathered around her now confused her. *Why are they all being so nice to me?* she asked herself. *Hey it's me,* she mocked silently. *Seducer of the pastor's innocent son . . . me, who got hit by a car for her sins . . . hello? They must remember everything, especially the cursing I gave that idiot pastor's boy when I realized he wasn't coming with me, the day I walked out of here.*

Perhaps they had forgiven her. After all, they were supposed to be forgiving Christians. But were these smiles and kind words – imbued with love and compassion – genuine? She wanted to believe they were.

Lauren let her guard down. She smiled, losing herself, indulging in the fuss around her.

In front of her, near the pulpit, the Soul Seekers beefed up the bass as sunshine glimmered through the building. The choir's pristine blue gowns swished from side to side as they clapped to the music. They smiled as they sang.

Lauren swayed with the rest of the throng as the band began in earnest, singing along to old gospel choruses almost pepped up to dance-hall standards. Joy was already lost in the rhythm, clapping her hands, eyes closed. Her face held the same serene expression as last night, only then she'd been dancing slowly, puffing a joint, joined at the groin with the best looking man at the party. And now here she was at church. Joy had explained it to her once: 'My relationship with God is personal. What I do is between my God and me.' *I wish I could be a bit more like her*, Lauren thought. *I'd love to just step between two worlds and be accepted by both.*

Whether it was the music, the atmosphere, the genuine warmth she felt from people or just nostalgia, something triggered dormant memories. Feelings she'd had when she was a bona-fide member of the church. To her surprise she began to cry. Those were the good old days. All she'd had to do was play by the church's rules and abundant love and friendship were hers. She missed that sense of close-knit community.

Joy looked over, concerned. She nudged Lauren. 'Sermon starting,' she whispered.

As the minister took to the pulpit, the music ground to a halt with all the subtlety of a stylus ripping across a record. People sat quietly. The minister began his sermon calmly; a warm-up for the fire and brimstone performance they all knew was coming. Lauren disengaged, thinking of the previous night's party.

She was brought back to the church by a familiar twitching in her limbs. Her medication was wearing off. She reached into her purse for her Diazepam. It would take a while to work. She bit her lip, a little scared. She could feel her limbs threatening civil war. She'd left it too long.

Whatever happens, they can't see me lose control, she thought. That would be way beyond embarrassment. She clenched her teeth and shut her eyes.

In front of the congregation, the preacher's microphone popped and screamed feedback as he worked himself into a verbal frenzy.

'Can I hear an amen!'

The congregation obediently roared a fearsome response. Lauren inhaled sharply. *Must relax, must let the tablets work.* She rocked gently, repeating her mantra. Bundles of muscles fought against her will.

'Ha ha! Satan can't get you. Praise the Lord with me!'

'Praise the Lord!' a hundred and fifty voices thundered. The noise startled Lauren and she held her arms close to her body. Her anxiety levels were dangerously high.

'Jesus has the victory! Stamp your feet and clap your hands if you agree!'

A sound like stampeding animals shook the floorboards. Lauren froze. Her muscles trembled.

'Raise your hands and say hallelujah if you love the Lord!' More feedback rebounded around the church, vibrating eardrums and chest cavities.

Lauren lost the battle. Her body jerked. The powerful muscles in her legs contracted, forcing her upward, out of her seat. 'Aargh!' she shrieked, arms waving to keep her balance.

The church saw Lauren's medicinal mismanagement and sudden outburst as a sign. The Spirit had moved through her sinful body. A floodgate of hysteria broke loose throughout the church. A woman near the front – hair expertly hot-iron curled under her broad hat – was the first. She was no lightweight but she began to jump up and down on the spot, screaming.

'Jeesuus, Jeesuus!' The woman's eyes were tightly shut, right hand waving to the sky. As she got into the Spirit her head shook from side to side, spinning her hat loose to reveal a squashed crown of uncombed hair.

Lauren and Joy stared at her. Lauren's muscles ached, but she felt a giggle threatening to burst through her lips. Joy pinched her playfully, then buried her head in her Bible.

'Woooy!' came a deep gutsy howl from the back of the church.

'A hallee . . . a hallee a halleeloooyah!'

The howls came in breathy succession, accompanied by stamping and hooting, as slowly, the sound moved closer to the front of the church.

The howling, hatless woman began to stomp down the aisle, punching the air. She slumped at the foot of the altar. Lauren cupped two more pills to her mouth. Eyes were shut, the congregation was alive with sobs and indecipherable words.

'Alamakashundah!'

'Eekalashundah!'

Lauren swallowed and held on to Joy, whose shoulders were shaking. 'Why does it all end with "shundah"?' she yelled over the din.

'Makalamshundah!'

The two friends collapsed against each other, overcome with stifled laughter.

Lauren smiled to herself as she straightened up. She used to have her own calling call whenever she got in the Spirit. *It wasn't like I had an out of body experience, like they all kept saying, I did it because I had to look as holy as my mates, Lerlene and Yvette.*

She watched as the church rolled, remembering the two women. They'd been champion babblers, speaking in tongues as soon as anyone said amen. She'd been so desperate to join the ultra pure, the only ones who could speak in tongues, that she'd made something up, remembered it, and yelled it out whenever things got a bit frenzied.

Speaking in tongues was the ultimate test of holiness, and Lauren couldn't bear the sorry looks and consolation people gave her when they heard she hadn't been *touched*, hadn't spoken yet. She'd become embarrassed by it. So she'd faked

37

it. So what? Hadn't they all been faking it too? Lerlene had been the best: she'd get wild, sobbing. She could give herself a snotty nose at will. They'd got baptized at the same time. Played along with the rules. No trousers, no make-up, no jewellery, no fancy hairdos, no cinema, no alcohol, no nightclubs and definitely no boys.

Heard she got pregnant too. Wonder what she's doing these days? Lauren thought.

Those not caught up in the moment sat composed, ignoring the mayhem. Joy sat still, her large almond eyes closed, fanning herself with a song sheet.

Lauren's muscles reasserted themselves, insistently twitching in opposing directions. She needed to get away from the noise, the chaos. Panic began to set in again. She took another pill and sat back awkwardly, waiting for it to take effect, willing her muscles to relax.

'Ooh yes, praise the Lord,' said the minister. He spoke quietly now. His flock began to calm down. Soothing chords from the piano ushered people back to their seats as they fixed their hats back on to ruffled heads, straightened their clothes into respectability.

'Everyone stand,' said the minister.

Lauren sat defiantly. Why did he think he had the right to order her about? No one cared about her needs, or her ability to stand.

'*Truly* the Spirit has visited us this morning,' the minister declared majestically. 'Let us give thanks.' He spread his arms. 'Each of you talk to Him and ask for healing to come down. Come to the altar those of you who are sick. You know that *sickness* is because of *sin*! Come let Him lift the burden of your sins and heal you. All you sinners out there who used to belong and have become backsliders, everything can be made right, just come, come to the altar.' His voice quivered as he spoke.

People stood and hummed along to the music. Some moved towards the altar. Lauren felt safe surrounded by the standing, praying mass. She took her mind off her panic by admiring the Sunday-best clothing around her. As the tablets released the tension in her muscles, her head felt pleasantly detached from her surroundings. Through the haze she heard the drones of fervent prayers spoken with passion and emotion. She began to drift, half asleep.

Then she heard the commanding voice of the minister calling her name.

'Come to us, dear sister Lauren, I have *healing* for you today! Come to the altar and claim what is *yours!*'

This can't be happening to me! Lauren thought. She could feel herself going numb with panic. Her nose began to sweat. She scrambled around in her coat pocket for a tissue.

'Come, sister Lauren! He is calling *your* name!'

Among her usual pocket debris of clumped old tissues, half strips of chewing gum, safety pins and fluff, Lauren's fingers stumbled across a tiny bottle of vodka, courtesy of the previous night. If ever she needed a drink it was now. She cloaked the bottle in her handkerchief and lifted it to her mouth. Anyone watching might have thought she was wiping her nose.

The white spirit spread its warmth out to her shoulders, down her arm and spine, untangling and relaxing bundles of tight muscles. She took another pill. She knew this was wrong, liquor and medication, but the preacher was looking at her expectantly. Two large women dressed in white moved towards her to help her from her seat. Resistance seemed useless; impolite, even.

All eyes were upon her. *Oh God, please let me at least walk normally*, she pleaded. But self-consciousness and fear contracted the muscles still untouched by pills and alcohol, throwing her shoulders forward and pulling her right foot inwards to face the left one. The formerly happy faces that had greeted her earlier now regarded her like a pitiful animal as she limped down the aisle, flanked by the women in white.

How could they trick me like this? She felt betrayed and stupid. She'd let her guard down. *I'm nothing more than good-will prey!* Angry and humiliated, she burst into tears.

The congregation took this as a sign of remorse, a sign that she was willing to give her soul to the Lord again. A sign that she admitted she was a sinner. They whooped in joy.

The women in white left her on the floor among the other praying, jabbering altar gatherers. They moved towards the minister, carefully dabbing his sweaty brow as he moved through the sea of bodies at the altar, placing his hands on heads, sending them one by one back to their seats.

Lauren crouched, swallowed two more tablets and listened to the wailing. Her whole body felt like a fireball. *Imagine God listening to this bloody racket every Sunday all over the world.* Despite everything, and with help from the pills and alcohol, she laughed to herself. *Reckon that's why there's so many earthquakes an' stuff, cos all this lot's given Him a headache and He's gotta let His own stress out.* She tittered, letting the effects of the little white pills wash over her.

The altar emptied until there was just the minister and Lauren left. He held her head with both hands and looked into her eyes.

'Do you believe the word?' he bellowed.

'Yes,' she squeaked.

'Do you believe He can take your sins away and make you *whole* again?'

'Yes,' she answered drowsily as the tablets relaxed her muscles.

'Then stand up straight for me, my child! Stand up and claim *victory* over Satan!'

Lauren wanted to dance. She was so high.

She sprung to her feet, posture perfect. The congregation gasped. As Lauren put one foot straight in front of the other hallelujahs went up, people clapped and broke into a gospel chorus, boosted up by the band.

Is it me or is this place spinning? she thought. She was beyond caring. It had been ages since she had taken pills and booze together, and she felt good. She wanted to dance. Like Joy danced. The heavy bass guitar begged her to swing her hips and stomp. She stomped. She put one foot in front of the other, added more hip movement. Stomp four, she began moving away from the altar. Stomp eight, she was clapping her hands in time with everyone else, dancing her way back to her seat.

There wasn't a dry eye in the church.

After ten more minutes of wailing and praying, the reverential cue of the piano silenced the church.

'What we have seen today is truly a miracle!' the minister breathed.

'Come on you, get your coat on.' Joy smiled as Lauren sat. 'It'll be a miracle if you don't fall asleep on the way home.'

The next afternoon Lauren's head ached when she got up. The answer machine was flashing two messages. The first was from Joy.

'Hey, Born Again Girl, just checking in to see if you're OK. You sure can sleep. You should be out spreading the word, like you promised the pastor.' Joy laughed.

Lauren shuddered, trying to recall the previous day.

The answer came with the second message.

'Sister Lauren, this is Pastor Brown.'

Lauren began to remember what had happened.

'I shall be coming over at four o'clock for a prayer meeting

41

to give thanks for your healing. Praise the Lord.'

She had promised to change her life, start anew, go back into the church. It had all been a mistake. *Why did I have to get so out of my head? Those people will never just accept me as I am. It's OK for Joy. She can come and go as she likes. How am I going to explain that I'm still disabled and not looking for a cure?*

After an hour of hard thinking Lauren jumped at the sound of her doorbell. Her heart thumped.

She greeted Pastor Brown through the intercom and told him to make his way to the living room. Then she made her entrance. Pigeon-toed, right arm contracted, shoulders hunched.

The minister's mouth dropped open. Before he could speak, Lauren began.

'Well, pastor, here I am again. Looks like that healing didn't take to me,' she said matter-of-factly. 'Do you suppose that if God is love, the lesson He is giving me is that I have to love myself as I am, stop trying to be perfect, and just get on with my life?' She thought of her favourite Bible verse, Matthew seven, verse one. *Judge not, that ye be not judged.* She began to laugh. 'By the way, how's your wife? Has her diabetes healed yet?'

She felt a new high run through her as the pastor's face sagged. Maybe she *would* enjoy church next Sunday. Perhaps she would wear Versace. Yes. Versace and bright red lipstick.

One Last Time

Kavita Bhanot

It's cream and maroon, his reply to my letter. Simple. Classy. Not like the cheap, tacky one they sent out for my Mamu's wedding. We both laughed at its painfully bright colours and festive gold glitter, at the off-the-boat moustached groom and the ghostly pale bride with demure and down-cast eyes. At least Sunny was allowed a say in this.

I open the card for the fifty-third time and mouth the words to myself.

> *Mr and Mrs Dutta request the pleasure of*
> *Meghna Kureishi*
> *on the auspicious occasion of the marriage ceremony of*
> *their beloved son Sunil Dutta and Sonali Sharma.*

I have to laugh at the idea of his parents requesting my pleasure. Sunny and I know why I was sent an invitation. Formality, I think you call it. I know he doesn't expect me to come. After all, the last thing he said to me was that he never wanted to see me again.

Sunil and Sonali. Even their bloody names go together. I

43

bet his parents took that into consideration as well. I finger the date: Sunday, 9 September 2001. It's like a dull pain you think you've forced out of your mind, until someone asks if it hurts. It's today's date.

Programme
10:00 *Reception of Baraat*
11:00 *Milni and Tea*
12:00 *Marriage Ceremony*

I glance at my watch. Sunny always kept his watch twenty-five minutes ahead of time. He was always late and he thought it might trick him into being on time. It didn't work. Instead he just added about half an hour to the time his watch showed, making him even later.

Eleven twenty-one. The families must be greeting each other with garlands right now. Appropriate, that – the families meeting first, it is a marriage of families. On second thoughts, his family probably hasn't even arrived yet. The schedule's superfluous because Asian weddings never run on time and the boy's family has to arrive late. It's part of a rich tradition and culture. I'm sure Sunny didn't have a problem with keeping that tradition either. I always said he'd be late for his own wedding.

I put the invitation back in the cupboard where it's been living. Maybe if it sits there I won't think about it. It helps. A little. Whenever I get a thank-you box of chocolates from one of my patients, I put it in the same cupboard so I'm not tempted to eat them all in one go. They last a couple of days.

Dropping on to the sofa, I flick through the TV channels, *Hollyoaks*, *Grange Hill*, some church service. I always knew that I'd never be able to marry him. How many times did I sit there, listening incredulously, while he explained that he'd never marry anyone of a different religion because it would upset things too much? I assumed he was talking about his parents. He was so keen on making his family proud; gave himself such a hard time if he didn't get an A for every exam and assignment. And he usually did. I barely scraped through my exams. God knows how I qualified as a doctor.

As long as I was around him, I pushed his opinions about marriage further and further towards the back of the cupboard until they became decayed and dusty – fit to be thrown away, as far as I was concerned. I began to hope. Then Sunny delved in and pulled them out, blowing away the dust and cobwebs and shoving them rudely in front of my nose.

'We went to someone's house over the weekend.'

'Oh yeah? Whose?'

'A girl's.'

I looked at him expectantly.

Pulling at moulting strings from the student sofa. 'You know . . . I told you my parents are trying to hitch me up, and –'

'Why on earth are you *letting* them arrange your marriage?' I interrupted. 'You're only twenty-three, for God's sake! You haven't even done your finals, you're too young to be thinking about bloody marriage.'

He looked up. 'Hey, keep your hair on. I didn't say I was gonna marry her. There's no harm in looking.'

Silence. The type that rings in your ears.

Nonchalantly. 'Well?'

'Well what?'

'Well, what does she look like?'

'She's . . . fit . . .'

'But . . .'

'But nothing. She seemed all right . . . you know, a nice person 'n' all that.'

'You know that, after meeting her for, like, half an hour?' I said scornfully. 'Anyway, what are you going to do with such a "nice person" if you can't even talk to her on your level, go out with her, introduce her to your friends?'

'What are you talking about? She's not from the goddamn village. She's lived here all her life. And she's not thick, she's a solicitor . . .'

'Lord of all hopefulness, Lord of all Joy . . .'

Singing intrudes into our conversation and I realize I've been watching the Sunday morning service. *Four minutes past twelve.* I try to imagine Sunny in the marriage ceremony; his forehead scrunched up in that nervous frown and his mouth twitching just like it did before his final-year presentation. He is clear, but the girl next to him is out of focus. Closing my eyes, I try harder to see her, but it's no use. She looks like me.

It suddenly strikes me that I'll never be able to visualize him with anyone else unless I witness his conviction with my own eyes. Unless I go to his wedding.

I've been toying with the idea ever since the letter bomb first landed on my doormat, twisting and turning it around in my head, trying it on, taking it off. I realize now what I guess I always knew: I need to go. I can give myself a hundred and one contradictory reasons why: to accept the marriage, to avert it somehow, to show that I don't care, to know that he cares . . . but they're all just words, empty words that can't express the feeling, the need.

I need to see him one last time.

Uninvited, his last words come creeping up behind and tap me on the shoulder. I shrug them off. He didn't mean it, he was angry at the time. Once he sees me he'll forget.

The decision made, I go through the motions of getting ready as if I've prepared for this many times before. I have in my mind. Straight for the midnight blue and silver silk sari I

46

'borrowed' from Mum when I last went home, just in case. I don Mum's silver earrings and necklace and enough make-up to make myself unrecognizable. I'm no longer the same person, but some other adult, sophisticated and in control. I feel safer in the mask; like a fencer's mask it will protect me from getting hurt.

I'm not conscious of how or when I get into my Peugeot and drive to the Rex Centre. It's only when I arrive that my resolve begins to melt. Watching myself walk down Coventry Road, I wonder what I'm thinking of. I used to make fun of those dumb horror-movie stars, the ones that walk right into the haunted house to investigate strange noises, instead of running out of the surrounding forest as fast as they can. Adjusting my sari, heart beating, I go in.

The overdressed hall seems a lot smaller than it actually is because it's teeming with a colourful pick 'n' mix of people. Shapely cola bottles mingle with their superior counterparts, the shapely milk bottles. Flying saucers, fat and flat, are watched critically by bubblegum eyeballs, while floating lips indiscriminately peck at scarlet strawberries. Standing in the doorway, I notice a division in the gathering. On one hand, there are those who are actively involved, rushing around importantly, proudly preoccupied and busy – whether they're mingling with other guests, or making some arrangement essential to the smooth running of the function. Everyone seems to know who they are and they know everyone. Almost. Then there are the many distant friends and relatives that nobody knows. Perched at tables, muttering the odd word to one another, they mostly look blank and bored. Their faces light up if anyone approaches them, even if it's simply to collect their rubbish. As I approach them, they note the arrival of another miscellaneous guest with interest. I take a seat in the stalls.

I look round for Sunny but it's hard to see anything

through the opaque flurry of activity. Centre stage, I spy a sort of canopy, lavishly decorated in red and gold. It covers half the population of the hall and all the action. He must be under there too, but my efforts to catch a glimpse of him through a gap between the auntie-jis are unsuccessful. Damn. People walking past are blocking my vision. I look at their faces and realize that they used to be my friends. Before we can pretend not to have recognized one another, it's too late. They come over and offer stiff greetings, their shock covered by masks of politeness. Soon there's nothing left to say and they walk away. I nibble at a lone, cold samosa, trying to pluck up the courage to seek him out. I just need to see him one last time.

I stand up resolutely and stride forward before I lose my nerve. Halfway down the hall, I feel my sari pleats falling out – this is not the way one is supposed to walk in a sari. I look around for the sophisticated, controlled adult I saw earlier in front of my mirror. Failing to find her, I search for an escape instead and head for the toilets. Standing before the mirror, trying to make sense of my sari, I notice the reflection of two teenage girls in a similar predicament.

'Don't you think Sonali looks gorgeous? I can't wait till I get married and have such a fuss made of me.'

'Are your parents gonna find you someone?'

'No way! I'm not marrying some boring accountant from Leicester. Mind you, Sonali's pretty cool.'

Surprised now. 'What, your parents arranged your brother's –?'

'Well, my parents introduced them and – Does that look all right? Could you pin it for me? – and then they spent more than a year getting to know each other. My parents were getting worried because he wouldn't say yes for ages.'

'Why do you think that was? Was he going out with some-one else?'

'No, I don't think so. We did get a letter sent us by some girl. Sunil had never mentioned her but she claimed she was having his kid, that they'd been together for years. She told Mum and Dad they couldn't force Sunil to marry Sonali, because he wanted to marry *her* and couldn't because she's Muslim.'

'But your parents still made him marry –'

Heading towards the door. 'That's just it, it wasn't true. Sunil told us that he'd never gone out with her, he hadn't even' – she giggles – '*done* it with her. They were mates, but he never fancied her. She was obsessed with him and had it in her head that there was something between them.'

'She sounds crazy . . .'

Snickering. 'Yeah, something like that . . .'

She sounds crazy.
   Something like that.
   She sounds crazy.

The words spin around and around in my head, making me dizzy. Memories thrown in the blender; fragmented images of staying up all night to help him finish his essay when I hadn't even started mine; of once again cancelling plans to go out with friends because he was feeling down. I only ever tried to be a good friend, to help him. And he thinks I'm obsessed?

Then the truth occurs. *Of course.* He had to let his parents think that. He always had a weak spot for them, said he could never hurt them. He wasn't strong enough to stand up to them, to grab the lifeline I threw out to him.

I go back in the main room. I just need to see him one last time.

The ceremony is over and the crowd has dispersed. He's sitting on a throne and I wonder why I feel the same tremor on seeing him that I always have. Surely something should

49

have changed. He's a married man now. She's sitting next to him. His wife. She whispers something in his ear and he laughs. Happy. He looks at her with a tenderness in his eyes that I craved for three years. Then his glance falls on me. And . . . nothing: no anger, no hatred, no emotion. A stranger on the street.

He doesn't love me. He never has and never will. I need to move on, let go. That's what everyone tells me.

And I will . . .

Twelve seventeen.

My arm reaches out to open the cupboard door.

I just need to see him one last time. I have to go to the wedding.

Grandfather's Feet

Barrington Gordon

My grandfather's feet lied to me.

As a child, I'd sat at his feet, fascinated by them. They were not as men's feet should be, but as soft as butter. This was very strange; my grandmother complained about how hard her feet were, said that they shouldn't be rougher than his because Grandad walked many more miles than she did. But he still had softer feet. I couldn't understand why.

The contours of his feet were smooth. Prominent veins drew a miniature map that I traced with delicate fingers as I helped him to wash them. I felt great joy as I played with them, using his blue sponge to lather the soap, squeezing suds over them from high up. As the soap slid down and dissolved on the skin, unusual star shapes formed and then melted away back into the bowl. He loved watching me search for them. We sat in front of the coal fire, smoke coupling with flames to create an array of dancing silhouettes that kept me entertained for hours. There were fire horses, dogs, butterflies and devils, all in that hearth. If I got scared I clung to Grandad's feet and he reassured me.

His feet were beautiful, but even then I knew they lied,

51

held secrets, ones that I wanted to unlock. Surely his life couldn't have been as easy as he made out. My grandfather was a giant of a man with very gentle ways, yet he was shrewd and determined in the face of whatever cards life dealt him. He believed it was not for us to question life but to subjugate ourselves to it and do good in all situations. His smiling eyes, quiet but confident, were looking at me.

'Do good, Daniel,' he always said, patting my five-year-old back with his large, spade-shaped hands. His touch made me smile and a warm feeling would grow inside me, knowing that Grandad trusted me. No matter what happened, just the thought of my grandfather made it feel all right.

I'd placed the phone back in its cradle and tried to come to terms with what my grandmother had just told me. My grandfather was dead.

'Come home, come, he dead.' I could still hear her voice. Its tone told me that she was holding back the many things that she wanted to say.

I shivered: someone was screaming. Before I knew it, I was down on the floor, wrestling, trying to control the grief. *How dare they scream?* I thought. It was my grandfather who was dead. Then I looked in the mirror and realized that it was me making that noise. Me! The house was empty. The noise stopped as suddenly as it had begun. I stood there, hands over my own mouth.

Later, much later, when he lay before me in his coffin, stretched out for all to see, questions assaulted my mind. Why had he been so disappointed in me? Guests mingled round, friends whom I hadn't seen for years. Friends – the word felt awkward in my mind, it seemed to grow inside my brain, making it hurt. How could they really be my friends? I didn't know them and they didn't know me. What they held in their minds was a childhood memory of me. I wanted to shout at them, to say that they didn't know who I was, that I was someone different now: I'm not the sixteen-year-old who left home eighteen years ago!

My life hadn't worked out. At thirty-four years old I was divorced with a son who hardly spoke to me. The divorce had been bitter and my grandfather hadn't approved of how I'd handled things, especially with his great-grandson. Consequently, Grandad and I hadn't spoken for some time. Now it was too late. I'd always thought there'd be time to make up. Perhaps one day my boy would decide to speak to me. He'd realize that his father was right.

I thought about my own father. They tell me I look like him. He and my mother were killed in a car accident on the way from visiting relatives in Wolverhampton. It's impossible for a three-year-old to understand when his grandmother says, 'Daddy and Mummy won't be coming back home.' I went to live with my grandparents in Lozells. As far as Grandad was concerned, I was his son. It felt so reassuring to have a dad again.

Over the years, my grandfather walked miles to feed his family. The paths he frequented were slippery and would have challenged even the most sure-footed. My grandmother told me how, during the 1960s, he trudged through deep snow – I imagined it reaching up to his waist.

'Bwoy,' he would bellow, in that gravelly, familiar voice, 'if you was out there today wit me you fingers would freeze! It frost up out there. That snow' – he pointed through the dining-room window – 'sharp enough to cut you skin.' He slipped off the two layers of gloves that had done a poor job of keeping his hands dry and I looked at his fingers, resculpted by the cold and snow into claw shapes.

My grandmother brought in a bowl of warm water for his hands. She stood in front of him, restyling her hair into a bun, fastening it with hairpins produced from her apron pocket and held poised between her lips. I thought of a kangaroo's pouch. Was Grandma a kind of kangaroo? Gently, his cold hand pulled hers down.

'No . . . let yuh hair fall to yuh shoulders,' he said. He smiled that disarming smile. 'I don't get a chance to see yuh wit it down often.'

Grandma was a devout Christian and her church preached that women should not let their heads be unnecessarily uncovered. She began to protest – 'Pastor say . . .' – but before she could finish, my grandfather asserted himself.

'I marry yuh, not the pastor.'

She couldn't resist him. She smiled and took out the hairpins. Her hair fell down – black shining locks unravelling, sitting on her shoulders. She looked beautiful and shy with it. She no longer looked like my grandmother.

Grandad looked like he'd been given a present. When he placed his hands in the warm liquid his wife had brought him I watched her soft face ripple with concern as pain gripped him. Gradually, life came back into his hands, but soon he was scratching as if he'd plunged them into itching powder. The more he scratched, the worse it got. His hands became swollen, covered with red blotches. Grandma was puzzled, then she realized what it was: chilblains. Grandad was in tears; his only relief was when Grandma put his hands under the cold water tap. I decided that snow was nice to look at but could hurt you. This kind of snow turned an ebony-coloured black man into blue steel.

As I grew older I looked forward to him coming home. I was at the ready with the white enamel bowl with the small bluish chip in it. I had chipped it one day when I'd filled it with too much hot water. The heat penetrated the bowl and my hands began to burn. I tried to rush to the dining-room fire without

54

spilling anything, but hot water scalded my legs and before I knew what was happening the bowl lay at my feet, chattering. The impact on the enamel made it crackle and continue to splinter as if it had a life of its own. Grandad came running into the kitchen. I was frightened, thinking he would be angry with me but he wasn't, he was worried that I'd hurt myself.

The next day Grandfather came home with marks on his face and his clothes torn. He worked at Longbridge making Minis, and his part of the factory was dominated by a group of Teddy boys who picked on him. Their hair was slicked back, their jackets long and colourful, and wedged shoes gave them extra height. Grandad had been told by Sylvia, a canteen lady, that one of their girls had teased her boyfriend with remarks about how handsome my grandfather looked in his winkle-picker shoes – he was the kind of man who liked to dress smart. When the factory whistle blew, Grandad left quickly to avoid trouble but in seconds he was being chased; he really had to run for his life. He boarded a bus but they got on too. Safe all the way to town, then they were after him again when he jumped off at Corporation Street. He sprinted towards the Town Hall, cut down by the canal, across Gas Street Basin and headed for Hockley. In no time he was back home in Lozells. His feet carried him to safety. Grandma pleaded with him to get a car, but he said he'd rather use the money to put food in his grandchild's belly.

I remember him arriving home one afternoon, sometime in the late 1960s. I was lying in front of the bright coal fire; my grandmother told me to move away from it because the heat was making me drowsy. I got up and wandered into the front room. Through the misty windows I looked out at the cold streets where deep snow held abandoned cars ransom. The world looked quiet, peaceful. That morning my grandmother had woken early and gone into her stark kitchen.

Its red quarry tiles looked warm, but were cold to the touch. I often sat in that kitchen and blew what I called cold bubbles, my breath mixing with the cold air, pretending I was in a cartoon. I watched my grandmother make my grandfather a Thermos full of 'love porridge'; she said it took all the love in the world to go into that freezing, red-tiled kitchen on a winter's morning.

Inside, I felt warm and protected; safe from the neighbours and the factory workers who hated my grandfather because he was a proud black man. He said they called him 'nigger' and 'wog'. It hurt me to hear this but he'd smile at the worried look on my face. When I asked him to tell me more he put a finger over his lips and said 'Shhh'. But on that afternoon he'd arrived home with blood on his face and a split lip. He tried to hide from me, but my grandma could not shield his towering body.

'Who hit you, Grandad?'

I clenched my six-year-old fists, ready to fight the unseen enemy. The warmth in his eyes assured me everything would be all right. He put me by his feet. I watched him soak and bathe them in the enamel bowl filled with soapy water as Grandmother kissed and cleaned his face.

Those were the good old days. After the telephone call from my grandmother I'd packed my belongings and headed for the train station. As I sat on the train the terrible argument we'd had, the one which had led to my departure, came sharply into focus. At sixteen, I was pining for my real father more and more. I was being bullied at school and didn't know how to tell my grandparents – I knew what they would say, Grandad's attitude seemed so old fashioned. His advice would be to turn the other cheek. As far as he was concerned, life brought us these challenges for a reason. His wisdom was no help to me in the schoolyard where racist slurs scattered around me like shrapnel. A distance had developed between us. One day he called me into the front room. Its polished, pristine state made me feel awkward: I was afraid to sit down, worried that I was going to dirty or spoil something. This room was out of bounds unless we had guests.

'Daniel?'

I looked up at him from the armchair, feeling tense.

'You been rude to yuh grandma again. What's going on?'

I didn't say anything because I didn't want to disrespect him. I thought my real parents would have understood but wasn't sure how to say so. The silence grew between us, stifling me. At last he spoke again and the tension in the atmosphere subsided.

'Those boys at school still giving you trouble, aren't they?'

I said nothing.

'You ain't got long left now, just try to hold on.'

I hated school and each day that I went through those gates was like going into battle knowing you were going to get beaten. I erupted.

'What do you know? You don't know what it's like to go in day after day and have kids ready to get you and the teacher don't care!'

He breathed out and nodded his head in despair. I realized how much he'd aged and I felt scared. One day he too would die and leave me. 'Anyway, you won't be around much longer,' I said. It came out all wrong, how it sounded wasn't how I'd meant it. I'd meant he would be at peace soon, without all this.

Grandad rose from his chair and the whole room seemed to shrink around him.

'Yuh out of order, likkle bwoy!' He grabbed me and started shaking me. Without thinking I lashed out just as Grandma came in to see what the noise was about. My grandfather let go and silence returned to the room. Grandma put her hand up to her cheek. Grandad's eyes filled with water. I

57

wanted to be anywhere except where I was at that moment.

'Get out!' were his only words as he left the room. I wilted into the armchair, trying to make sense of what had just happened. I heard Grandma rushing after him, begging him to forgive me. I sat there lonely and transfixed as the evening light darkened the room and hid my shameful tears. I didn't want to move from where I was.

Grandma came back in the room. I could tell she'd been crying.

'Daniel . . . you got to say sorry.'

I felt like no one understood me. I said nothing; I was scared I might insult her as well.

'He been through a lot to bring you up, yuh know.'

Still I said nothing, just watched her in the dark.

'Remember he told you how he used to like to run when you were a child? Why you think he stop?'

She fell silent. I felt the pressure to talk, but didn't. Eventually she left me to my thoughts.

When Grandad came to England in the 1950s his ambition was to be one of the first black men to run for England, the mother country. But his hopes were dashed when all he could get was work in the local steel factory. A heavy pipe fell on his foot, abruptly ending his dreams. The manager at the factory wouldn't let him have time off for the injury to heal properly and there was irreparable damage to his foot. But the only telltale sign that remained was a small scar, about half an inch long. You had to search for it.

I've seen many feet: gnarled, battered with awful skin, feet that have lost the war, hard skin almost fossilized, discoloured and riddled with veins that seem to cry out in pain. But my grandfather's feet . . . his had triumphed over the race of life.

Standing over his coffin I wanted to remove his shoes, to take one more look at his feet, and to ask him what it had really been like in those cold, harsh, unforgiving years.

The Darkest Hour

Yvonne Brissett

When I felt the round hard object in Leon's pocket, I thought
it was money. Ten pence, maybe. Then I felt the jagged edge.
I studied the key for a good hour before impulse took over.
It was a crazy idea, but I didn't care. Men were always messing me about. Time to switch the script. I knew where the
girl lived.

The key slid easily into the lock and I slipped quietly into
the house.

Tiptoeing along the gloomy hallway I tapped cautiously
on the first door on my right. It gave way to the slight pressure. I retched; dirty dishes, overflowing bin bags, ants all
over the place.

I blinked.

Holding my breath, I looked across to the adjacent room.
Yellowing newspapers. Broken toys. Crowded ashtrays. The
living room, perhaps. I could see the edge of a portable television in the corner, obscured by rubbish, then a settee pok-
ing out between piles of clothes.

I couldn't believe it. I had to be in the wrong place. Either
that or Leon must be losing it.

The staircase loomed before me. I hesitated, but couldn't leave without any evidence. I crept up the stairs, edging open the door straight ahead. The bathroom; nothing. I prodded the door to my left. The bedroom. A photograph stared back at me from the nightstand. Just one picture, that's all. Together. Hugging, smiling. I backed out of the room.

Then I heard her voice. High pitched. She sounded cheerful.

'Leon . . . I'm back. You still here?'

Oh shit. I moved back into the bedroom.

I scanned the room; nowhere to hide. How would I explain if she came up here?

It was quiet for a second, then a door slammed. She called again, closer now.

'Leon. I've done it. I made the appointment . . . you up there?'

Right, this was it. Should I hide or confront her? Confront? What was I *thinking* of? Here I was, in *her* house, after *sneaking* in, contemplating a challenge? I had to hide. My fingers felt under the bed. Forget that. It had a base. The wardrobe was full to bursting. The window! Thank God, an extension porch right below. Slates gave me easy access to the garden.

Trees provided shelter, blocking our view of each other when she leaned out.

Back home I studied a photograph of Leon and me. He'd looked so relaxed in *their* picture . . . or did he look happier with me? The harder I stared, the harder he stared back, hypnotizing me with those sexy eyes, sleepy under long lashes, and that toned physique, modelling six foot of smooth chocolate.

'He's a honey,' my friends said as soon as they saw him, just after we'd first met, about four months ago. 'But rather

The Darkest Hour

you than me. Pretty men are too much trouble, girls never leave them alone.'

He'd said: 'It's not who likes me; it's who *I* like that matters. I could have a hundred girls on my case, but unless they're you I'm not interested.' I'd grinned like an idiot and we'd fallen into bed.

I fingered the photograph, scrutinizing his face as if I might find some answers to the questions that plagued me. When did it all start? Why? What did she have that I didn't? It was little things that had got my mind racing in the first place – his mobile being switched off a lot, the way he some-times evaded my questions when I asked him where he'd been. I'd followed him late one night – he said he was pop-ping to the shop but instinct told me he was lying. It was too dark to see who opened the door. Now I knew why – no one had. He'd let himself in.

After that, I began to watch her. Mostly during the day-time, from a distance; sometimes crouched in doorways, at other times in bushes. I wanted to say something to him, but without proof I had no argument. Things were different now. I just needed the right moment.

I slipped the key back into his pocket, slumped down in the armchair, picked up the remote and switched on the tele-vision. Ricki Lake smiled eagerly at the camera, as if anticip-ating a few more steps up the ratings ladder.

'Today Natasha confronts her cheating boyfriend, Jamal. She's here to tell him it's over unless he dumps her best friend.' Ricki beamed with excitement. 'Yes, that's right. Natasha has *just* found out Jamal is seeing her *best friend* Monique behind her back!' Ricki turned to face Natasha. 'So, you're saying it's time for Jamal to shape up or ship out?' she asked.

'Damn straight!' pint-sized Natasha agreed. 'He bin doggin me for too long now an' I ain' takin it no mo,' she drawled, rolling her eyes and jerking her neck from side to side. 'We bin datin for ovah a year an' we's tight. Now he wanna be actin all strange. Don' wanna do nu-un wi' me an' I ain' goin out like dat.'

I shifted in my chair with growing interest. Maybe Ricki would bring on a therapist or a counsellor.

'Is it true he's cheating on you with your best friend?' Ricki questioned.

'Yeah. They be doin their thang . . . but you know what?' Natasha waved at the audience, showing off glamorous false nails, then slapped her hand across her chest and let it fall dramatically to her side. 'It stops right here, right now!'

'How did you find out they were seeing each other?' Ricki pushed.

'It don' take no brain surgeon to figuh it out. I bin ridin with Monique since we was kids. Hell! . . . I noticed how she be actin all defensive whenever I'm dissin *my* man and tryin to tell *me* how to love him right!' Natasha rocked with emotion. 'Anyway, I got her ticket . . . she gon get what's comin to her.'

'OK,' Ricki announced. 'Monique, come on out.'

A curvaceous teenage girl rushed on stage and marched over to Natasha, pointing in her face.

'Yeah. I'll take your man and I'll show him what a real woman's all about,' she yelled, running her hands over her sizeable curves.

Natasha jumped up and was promptly shoved back into her chair.

'Welcome to the show, Monique. Why would you do a thing like this to your best friend?'

'Oh, so it's like dat is it?' She eyed Natasha. 'Ain' you told em what you did to me? How you messed wi' not one but *two* of my boyfriends back in the days?'

As the audience gasped, Ricki piped up, 'Natasha, is this true?' Natasha sunk into her chair. An uncomfortable silence hung in the air. 'Let's hear what Jamal has to say,' Ricki said, eyes wide.

With his long plaits, deep dimples and cheeky smile, Jamal slunk on to the stage and sat down between the two girls.

He flung his arms up. 'Hell, I'll take em all on!' He grinned and the catfight began.

'So in fact, Natasha,' said Ricki condescendingly, 'it's you who dissed Monique first . . . and, Jamal, you just wanna be a player and you, Monique, think it's right to take your best friend's man? Well, what goes around comes around . . .'.

Hold on a minute. Wasn't it Ricki's role to encourage harmony and offer positive advice? Show how to improve self-esteem? Introduce an expert? Instead the woman thrived on her guests' humiliation, gloating about her loving husband, happy family and safe, perfect world. I needed advice – but she wasn't even worth watching. More to the point, it was nearly six. Leon would be home from work soon. I went into the kitchen and began preparing his favourite: ackee and saltfish.

'So how was your day? What you been up to?' He greedily tucked into his dinner.

'This and that.'

'Didn't you go out anywhere?'

'Just to the shop,' I lied.

'What about the careers centre? Nicole, I thought you said you were going job hunting?'

'I'll go tomorrow after I sign on. Anyway, how was your day?'

'Busy. Didn't stop. Everyone who came in wanted *me* to cut their hair. Queues all day.'

'You shouldn't be so popular then, should you?'

'And you shouldn't be so lazy. Just make sure you reach the careers centre tomorrow.'

I felt a pang of jealousy. I'd been in Leon's barbershop, HEADZ, a couple of times, had witnessed his skills. At a recent African-Caribbean Hair and Beauty show he'd picked up yet another award. This time for creativity. Then from nowhere, girls . . . flirting with him. He seemed to know them all. I didn't know any of them. With his talent it was no surprise that at just twenty-three he already had his own business. And here was I, fresh out of university with a journalism degree, struggling to get work experience. How could he even begin to imagine how that felt?

I dived out of bed. Three o'clock! No way. I couldn't believe it. I should have been at the job centre two hours ago. I sprinted down the Bristol Road and jumped on the 61. As usual, every single traffic light was red. It always happens when I'm in a hurry. People getting on or off at each stop, the driver slowing to give way to cars and other buses. I sighed – if I didn't make it in time, I'd be broke for days. As the bus drifted along I began to rehearse something to say to Leon later. I'd wanted to speak to him last night, but he'd been in such a good mood that I couldn't spoil it. Plus, how could I explain where I'd got my evidence? Somehow, a confession about stealing a key from *his* pocket and sneaking into *her* house didn't feel like the best starting point.

I decided to text him. I reached for my mobile and entered a few words. *I know what's going on. We need to talk.* No – too dramatic. Didn't sound right. I cleared the screen, dug around in my bag and pulled out my favourite book, *Acts of Faith* by Iyanla Vanzant. This collection of motivational sayings was like a bible to me. I carried it everywhere, consulted it for advice and inspiration. I ran my fingers along the index, found the word 'jealousy' and turned to the relevant page. 'When you strengthen your self-esteem there is no room for jealousy . . . jealousy is the surest way to get rid

64

of the very person you are afraid of losing . . . when you remember who you are, the jealousy will dissolve,' I read.

She was right. I needed to concentrate on me, to focus.

I glanced out the window. A stunning girl strutted past – the image of Iman. I thought back to the night of that last hair show, those girls. At home I'd asked Leon who they all were. He'd vaguely mumbled something about his 'bredrin's people' and changed the subject. I hate this kind of shady behaviour. I'm paranoid enough as it is without him acting like some secret service agent. My mobile rang. I hesitated when I saw the number.

'Yeah yeah.' Leon sounded like he was in the middle of a conversation.

'You all right?' I tried to sound chirpy.

'Yeah. You haven't cooked, have you?' he asked.

'No. I woke up late. I'm just on my way to sign on now.'

'Well, don't worry about cooking tonight. I'm gonna link up with the mans and play some pool and that straight after work, so I'll get something from the food shop.'

'OK.'

Yeah right. More like linking up with Queen of the Cesspool. I could feel a tingle working its way through my veins, a thumping sensation in my chest, my head. That's when I knew. Even if I wanted to, I couldn't leave this alone.

Another attractive girl bounced on to the bus and sat in front of me. Things became even clearer. No wonder I couldn't work out what to do. I was looking in the wrong direction. *She* was the one messing about with *my* man. Why take it out on him? It was *her* I should be thinking about. It was so obvious – why hadn't I seen it before? After all, I'd been down this road enough times. Arguing with my man when all the time, it was the girl who was to blame.

I'll admit I ignored all the warning signals with my ex, Cory. Ignored his new image, his disappearing acts. I'd tried

65

to convince myself I was being paranoid, neurotic, over the top, until *she* came right up in *my* face telling me about why don't *I* leave *her* man alone? The time before with Mikey was just as bad. I'd bumped into some girls from his college in town. They'd casually mentioned how fit he was and asked me if he was still seeing that girl on his course. 'Sorry,' they said when they realized their mistake, 'we didn't know you two were together.'

Well, it wasn't happening again. Quite enough humili-ation for one lifetime. Time to get even.

I jumped off the bus as it pulled into Corporation Street and hopped on the number 9. It was now gone four and traffic was building up on Broad Street. As the bus crawled along I cursed silently. Quicker to walk, I decided, pester-ing the driver to drop me off right away. I rushed past women clicking along in sharp suits, well-dressed business-men off to important meetings, bouncers lolling in the door-ways of trendy bars. A white stretch limousine pulled up outside the Hyatt. I cut my eye, disgusted. It should be a crime to have a job centre in the heart of the city. All I could see was wealth and prosperity. Oh well, just you wait, I thought, if I can't make the news, I'll be the news! I smiled.

Cars going nowhere, their frustrated drivers edgy with road rage, brightened my day even more. At least I wasn't the only one with problems.

As I left the job centre, the security guard was locking up the careers office next door. I was fed up of going in there anyway. The last time, the advisor made me write down my hobbies, interests and skills as well as my education and asked how I felt they related to my career choice. Then he'd suggested I maximize my potential by reading specialist newspapers, writing speculative letters, using my contacts, applying for absolutely everything. He made his suggestions as if I was a child; just two minutes after I'd told him I'd been doing all those things anyway. Please, tell me something I don't know, I thought, wondering if he'd ever been unemployed. Then the idiot turned round and said if I hadn't managed to secure my ideal job within six months, then I might as well think seriously about a career change. Give up my dream? Everything I'd strived for? Why did I even bother?

Midnight.

Still no sign of Leon.

Two o'clock. I heard the door slam.

Then he was all over me, pulling the quilt off, blowing gently in my face, kissing my eyelids, nose, cheeks, lips, trying to see if I was awake. I pretended to be asleep. I wasn't in the mood. All night I'd racked my brain, thinking of ideas of what to do to *her*.

The smell of alcohol on his breath, the feel of his smooth fingertips tracing their way along my inner thigh.

I'd thought up a wicked plan.

I felt myself weakening, lips moistening, body relaxing, responding to his touch.

I knew exactly how to deal with it.

His tongue flickering behind my ear, now teasing on my neck.

Perhaps I should be celebrating. He would be in London so the coast would be clear. It would be a breeze.

With him naked, pressing against me, kissing, caressing, soft lips everywhere, I melted into him, wanting him so badly, feeling his hands roaming between my thighs.

I slept peacefully.

'It's *next* Saturday? I thought the hair show was today?' He was still in bed.

'Nah, next week.' He moved the quilt out the way, revealing muscle. Regular weight training, football and martial arts gave him a body built to last. 'I'm only working this afternoon, so we can stay in bed a bit longer.' He winked, irritating me. Nothing like a well-laid plan ruined before I even had a chance to get it off the ground.

'So what you doing this weekend then?' I wanted him out the way.

'Well, tonight I'm all yours. Tomorrow evening I'm gonna go and check my bredrin Leighton. Remember him? The guy I introduced you to at that garage dance in London. The night when the Dreem Teem and Heartless Crew were playing and the place was ram with nuff Birmingham heads? I've heard he's moving to Bristol soon, so I'm gonna pass round.'

I wondered where he was really going. If he was going to see *her*. Either way, it didn't really matter. I'd just have to take the risk and do it then.

As soon as he left for work I jumped on the 45 into town and headed for the cashpoint. I knew my giro would take a few days to clear, but I was sure I had at least ten pound in there. As the crisp note slid out, my pulse raced. Time to start putting my plan into action.

I walked towards the old Bull Ring and headed for the new indoor market. I hoped the hardware stall was still around. So much was changing with all the redevelopments. This place, once so familiar, was a maze. Thankfully, I found the stall. I wasn't sure what I was after.

The market trader adjusted his cap, scratched his chin, rummaged through a box and produced a selection of items.

''Ere y'are, bab. Just what yer looking for. Any o' these should be foine.'

'So . . .' I held up one of the products, examining it. 'Is this one of your bestsellers, then?' I kept talking, introducing hypothetical situations to squeeze out any useful information. He seemed glad of the opportunity to delve into the less-visited corners of his brain.

As soon as I got in, I went online. Time to do a bit more research. I read Leon's e-mails, spent an hour in my favourite singles chat room, then tapped in www.google.co.uk and entered the key words. This was one of the best search engines. There must be something I could find out.

An hour later I had an idea of the basics, but it wasn't enough. I logged off, checked my watch. Four forty-five: a bit of time left. I flicked through the Yellow Pages until I found the right section. So many to choose from. Which one would suit me? Maybe I'd try a few. I picked up the phone, dialled the number and waited.

'Hello,' I said in my best distressed voice. 'I wonder if you can help me . . .'

Sunday evening Leon stayed in. We'd had a great weekend making love. He said he was worn out, didn't feel like going anywhere. Plus, his belly was too full. He'd cooked us a wicked dinner earlier. Rice and peas, jerk chicken, sweet potato candy and homemade coleslaw. He even made my favourite drink, pineapple punch. It was probably for the best he stayed in anyway. At least I knew he wasn't *there*. I told him I was popping out to a friend's. He was glad to see me making the effort, often mentioned that I didn't bother with my friends any more. It was true that since I'd moved in with him I'd seen less and less of them. But he didn't understand: it's no fun seeing all your friends in successful careers and happy relationships when you've got nothing.

I headed straight for hers. Just off the Pershore Road. That really got to me. Not only was he playing away, but right on our doorstep. Everyone must be laughing at me. But we'll see who has the last laugh. I rounded the corner. The streets were deserted. Only one streetlamp working, right at the other end of her road. Good – nice and dark. She was in: her lights were on and there was her baby. A gleaming Ford Focus. How could someone live in that kind of mess and drive such a spanking car?

It didn't take very long. I slipped on some old gloves I'd found at the bottom of a drawer, took off my rucksack and got out the torch, hammer and centrepunch. I approached the rear of the car and crouched down beside the back wheel. I looked right under and spotted the pipes the mechanic at the garage had described yesterday when I'd rung and said that my brakes were faulty. It's great playing the damsel in distress – amazing how men rise to the challenge, adopt these macho 'to your rescue' personas. It's even more fun when you humour them: act pathetic, play dumb, ask questions like 'What if someone's tampered with my brakes?' and 'How easy is it to damage them?' Under that spell, they start telling you all sorts, always starting, 'Well . . . I shouldn't really be telling you this . . . but . . .' It had worked like a dream.

I had no problem reaching under the car. The pipes went off to the left and the right. With the torch on the ground to illuminate the spot, I gripped the centrepunch firmly, positioned it, held it against the brake pipes and then hit it with the hammer. Not too hard, though. I remembered the mechanic's words: 'Just enough for the brake fluid to start seeping out.' After blabbing to me for ages he'd finally said, 'Pop it into the garage Monday morning. I'll take a look at it.' Funny. He should be telling her that, not me. I laughed gleefully, quickly packing away my tools. How would he feel if he knew he was involved in a conspiracy? You could almost call him my accomplice. Things were shaping up nicely.

Fifteen minutes later, I was wrapped up with Leon on the sofa. He was watching television, when I crept back into the house. And he had the stereo on full blast – hip-hop beats vibrating throughout. As I switched off the system, he pulled me down to play fight on the sofa, wrestling with me for distressing his vibe, his lazy eyes scanning me.

'How comes you're back so quick?' He kissed my neck. 'Not that I'm complaining.'

'She wasn't in.' I grabbed the television remote, flicking like mad. Perfect. He was distracted and began laughing at a clip on *Tarrant on TV*.

Monday couldn't come quick enough. Leon had gone to work. He'd left around seven – wanted to do some paperwork. I got up as soon as he left, showered, sat down in front of the mirror and reached for my make-up bag. It had been a long time since I'd worn any. Everyone said I didn't need it, thanks to my clear caramel complexion. But today was special. Time for the full works. I began applying it carefully. Foundation. Eye shadow, three shades. Eyebrow pencil. Liquid eyeliner. Mascara. Lip liner. Lipstick, two shades. Lipgloss. Blusher. I hardly recognized myself, but I liked what I saw.

I smoothed my hair, or should I say 'the' hair. I'd gone to hell and back to get this hairstyle. I bought the hair from the black hair shop under the Pallasades, cost me sixty pound. Real human hair is always more expensive than synthetic. Then another hundred and twenty pound to get it weaved into my hair at the salon. Now I had that African-American look, just like the model in the latest issue of *Today's Black Woman*. Smooth, sleek extensions, graduated and bobbed just below my shoulders. Leon always cussed me, calling me a joker, going to all that trouble then never bothering to tong, wrap, moisturize, oil, or in fact do anything with it, for full effect. Today would be different. Even he would be proud. I plugged in the tongs. Thirty minutes later, I held one mirror in front and one at the back of my head and admired my hair from all angles. It looked propa. I was beginning to feel empowered. I put on a CD, my Versace jeans, D&G leather biker jacket and new snakeskin boots with pointed toes and stiletto heels. Christian Dior's J'adore added the finishing touch.

I eyed myself approvingly in the mirror as Jill Scott's soulful lyrics filled the room – 'Getting In The Way' – well, this other girl's getting in the way of what *I'm* feeling.

'You go, girl!' I yelled, spinning round. I looked stunning, courtesy of Leon's hefty salary. I couldn't understand it. We got on so well together. That's why him cheating just didn't make sense. Well, if she knew who I was, even if she only caught a quick glimpse, I'd definitely give her something to remember.

I left the house. It was nine thirty a.m. I made my way to the bus-stop and waited. That day at her house, looking for somewhere to hide, I'd heard her say the appointment was at ten o'clock this morning in the city centre. It wouldn't be long before she'd be on her way. She'd have to drive past me – the other direction led out of town.

I leaned against the lamp-post and listened to the cars beeping. Men peered out of their windows to get a closer look at me. They made me sick – most of them must've had wives at home. Two bus drivers stopped and chided me for loitering at bus stops. The third simply chatted me up. Quite pretty. Nice dreads. Angry passengers complained, urging him to drive on and sparing me the usual drivel.

That's when I saw her coming towards me. Doing about forty. Her metallic, silvery blue car was instantly recognizable. I poised, trying to look as sexy, independent, confident and got-it-going-on as possible. The car drew nearer.

72

And then I saw him.

Right there, in the passenger seat.

Leon.

I panicked, flagging her down frantically. Leon noticed me, my arms flailing. He nudged her, was he trying to get her to stop?

The car hurtled on.

I looked on helplessly as they approached the roundabout. I started running towards them.

Maybe it's not her car? Course not; hers was definitely a darker blue.

Now a van coming from the opposite direction, fast. Don't be silly, I thought, Leon's at work, probably cutting hair right now.

The van . . . speeding. Easy mistake to make, it can't be them. Why was I running? I stopped. No, please . . . stop . . . the van.

It wasn't going to give way.

'She can't brake!' I screamed.

The car smashed into the side of the van. The van swerved out of control and began to roll.

Someone was holding on to my arm. A middle-aged woman with kind eyes. 'You've been hyperventilating,' she told me. 'You sure you're awroight, love?' she asked. 'Did you know them people in that car?'

I pulled my arm away. 'No. I'm fine,' I said and stumbled off.

How long was I rocking in the chair? Two hours? What had I done? It was on the news, just. No survivors. The phone rang. Could it be his mum? How could I speak to anyone? What could I say? But the noise was driving me crazy. I snatched up the receiver.

'Hello?' Tentative.

'Nicole, I've got some bad news.' It was Tia, Leon's favourite sister and a good friend of mine. She sounded shaken.

'What's happened?' I wanted to scream, pull out my expensive hair, confess, tell her everything.

'It's Leon.' Her voice broke. 'He's been in a car accident . . .'

'Oh my God. Is he all right?'

'There was nothing anyone could do . . .' she whispered.

Almost midnight. Crumpled in the same chair, I clutched fragile strands of tissue. I could still see the images and the thoughts kept on coming. They wouldn't go away. One after another. Finding the key. How I'd felt that day when I went round her house. How I'd tried to ignore my feelings. How much I'd wanted to confront Leon, but couldn't pluck up the courage. How much I couldn't bear to lose him. If I could've just *thought* about what I was doing, paid attention to what I had, appreciated it. It was *my* problem that I didn't trust Leon. Not his or hers. Mine. I should have spoken to him, communicated. Tried to break through the barrier of silence he often put up. His secretive attitude made it so difficult for me to talk to him sometimes. It had seemed the only solution – to frighten her. I thought the car would just skid out of control or something. The mechanic *said*. He said. He did. Dealt with punctured brakes all the time. Punctured brakes. Not this. Not death. I held my head in my hands and squeezed. What had I done?

A ringing. The doorbell. *Ignore it*. I wasn't expecting any-one. It was late. It rang again and again. *Stop!* I got up and tried to peep through the curtain without being seen. Our eyes locked. Tia.

'You look terrible,' she said. 'You can't just stay in here by yourself, crying like this. You gotta come round to my mum's. I told you to come. Everyone's round there.'

I sobbed in her arms. My regret, my guilt, my shame and stupidity dampened her top.

'It happened just before ten this morning,' she explained. 'They're not sure what caused it yet. He was with our cousin, Chanté, in her car. I know you haven't met her yet, but well, she's got, I mean she *had* mental health problems . . . been through a lot over the last few years; depression, schizophrenia. I think the final straw was when she lost her kids. Two cute girls, only three and four . . . in care now. We tried to stop it but there were problems with social services.'

Tingles began in my fingertips, crawling up my arms.

'Leon was the only one in our family she'd really talk to,' Tia continued. 'Her parents tried, bought her that new car last month to try and lift her spirits.'

The tingles worked their way along my spine, my collarbone, into the base of my neck.

'She didn't live far from here. Just round the corner in fact. Leon went there quite a lot. To try and help her, you know, talking to her. I know he'd been there even more these last few weeks because he was trying to get her moved.'

The tingling sensation was eating through me.

'He wanted to introduce you to each other ages ago, but Chanté made him promise not to tell you about her until she felt a bit better. She was making progress, what with the medication and everything, so he persuaded her to make an appointment with a specialist. He was quite good at motivating her like that.'

A thumping pain now, in my chest, my head.

Tia was still speaking. 'They were on their way to this appointment when it happened. Chanté was starting to look forward to meeting you, still a bit nervous, but excited – you know how Leon always sang your praises to everyone. He was hoping to introduce you two this week . . .'

75

I sat there, motionless. Everything was a blur.

My mum always said you never know how deep a puddle is until you step in it.

Later, I stared out the window. It was five a.m. and darkness stretched for miles. As I stood there alone, looking down, one thing became clear. The hour before daybreak is always the darkest hour. Only it dawned on me too late.

Shadow People

Martin Glynn

For the brotha who never made it

I'm sitting in a dreary, sparsely decorated flat, twelve floors
up, in a tower block in Newtown. Home is a sprawling mass
of concrete, a pissed-up lift that seldom works; we call it
Muggers Paradise. Single-parent mothers with attitude and
no man parade their trophies every day like a police line-
up, trying to guess who the fathers are. We're all living on
top of each other, submerged in a thick soup of inner-city
noises: couples fighting, hip-hop competing with garage, a
dog howling to be let out. Helicopters sweep over, looking
for some drugged-up joyrider that bent his last nicked car
round a tree before running into my block. Smells! Fucking
smells: shit, piss, bacon, overpowering perfume, weed, plus
the worst stench of all – poverty. I hate it. Every stinking
moment of it. All in the name of urban regeneration. I used
to think experiments were things that happened during
chemistry lessons. School. Seems like years ago. Twelve, to
be exact. It's just a blur now. Breakdowns kill off memory
like that – not that I want to remember anything – but nice

thoughts are good when you can get them. I used to have nice thoughts. Weather, clothes, my favourite meal. I have no sense of time now. I'm attached to the ceiling, looking down at myself. I don't belong down there with me.

The place is a tip. Last night's Chinese meal, a half-smoked spliff, cans of lager congregate on the floor. A small shaft of daylight pokes through permanently drawn curtains while I, Linton Jefferson Stephens, a dishevelled, mashed up black man wearing a ripped vest and boxer shorts lie face down in my own vomit. Thank God it didn't land on my vinyl. I always try and project sick downwards. I'm not always that lucky, though. A treasured Coltrane box set got it the other day. The whole set, ruined! I knew I should have bought CDs . . .

Deafening, disjointed sounds reverberate inside my head, making me dive into the corner of the room, shaking, rocking backwards and forwards, whimpering like a scared child. My breathing is erratic as another palpitation sets in. Sometimes I wish my tired heart would stop. But I'm not brave enough to do anything about it. So I wait to see when death will come and meet me face to face. I've always wondered if it's male or female. Does death wear clothes? Have a face? Be dread if death were black. Who cares? I just wish it would hurry up.

I pan around my room and focus attention on *that* photograph. I pick it up and stare, not wanting to look, but knowing I have to. The police told me she'd been raped. Was that before or after the eight stab wounds? I had to identify the body. It wasn't her. This photograph is her. We were gonna get married, have kids, settle down. We'd had an argument that day and I stormed out. She was so beautiful. I can still smell her skin. Sandalwood. She always used sandalwood, mixed with almond oil. I'd smear it all over her body and rub it in before we made love. We never had sex. We always made love. It's something that she insisted on. I protested at first, but in the end it worked out better. And now, what do I get? Advice. People trying to second-guess. 'Move on,' they tell me. 'It gets easier,' they say.

Where's God now? Where are my friends?

I go to the window, look out, then turn away, unable to deal with the glare from the light. I shut the curtains again, blocking out every beam, then plunge back to the safety of my corner. Here comes the manic, crazy laughter, then tears. Sometimes waterfalls, other times a small shower. I throw myself on to my back and stare at the ceiling, light a spliff. I take the biggest pull I can. I'm watching myself. Surrounded by the acrid smoke, smells sweeter than sandalwood right now. I draw the smoke deep into my mouth, letting it penetrate my lungs. It hits the spot. I moan and sigh, inhale again. Four days without sleep can be punishing, especially on the eyes. So I sit and wait for the night to come.

Most people fear the night, but it fascinates me. I'm consumed with its form, its total being and its majesty. I'm addicted to its mystery. Darkness lets me escape, hide among the shadows. Unseen and deadly.

Out of the blanket of darkness comes a powerful silence, broken only by the beautiful sound of a whispering breeze that stalks the lonely streets. I like the touch, the taste and the smell of the cool black night. It engulfs me from head to foot. The darkness is my friend, night is the messenger. They never let me down.

I get to my feet and retrieve her photograph. I stare at it again, wishing for it to come alive, to provide me with some peace of mind, some love, some hope. I gently place it back on the windowsill and peek through the curtain. The inner-city skyline looks great from a high-rise vantage-point until you see the sights close up. Tiny dots move beneath me. Shit always looks good from a distance. That's the way I like it. Distance, mileage, space. I watched them shoot a guy the other day. A young drug dealer who tried to go too far. That's what it's like, you try to occupy a little space, but someone either wants to take it away or set up stall on your patch. It was over so quick. The murderers scattered like running ants. That's when I shut the curtains. Up here you don't feel anything. It's like those guys in Vietnam who dropped the bombs. If you ain't on the ground it don't affect you. Or is it that I just don't feel any more? Who knows? Who cares?

My grimy bathroom. The place I come to freshen up. Never decorated it, never intend to. What's the point? You can't see new paint in the dark. This place has no feeling or character. Scrooge would feel at home here. A lone candle stands guard over the soap and toothpaste. I stare hard into the wall mirror, pulling stupid faces, then splash water on my ageing skin. Wonder how and why it all went wrong. I've lost count of how many rolls of toilet paper it's taken to patch up my battered hand – I keep having wall punch-ups – the hand I used to masturbate with. Even that has no meaning now.

Time for some relaxation. If you take my saxophone away, I'm dead. I blow, fondle, try to escape, remembering Coltrane. I begin to relax, then shit enters the right hemisphere of my brain. I retreat to the corner and start the whole goddamn ritual all over again. Got some friends this time. Tom and Jerry. I watch them try to catch each other out. Occasionally I join in, but usually end up smacking myself into a wall or falling over the furniture. They always disappear. One day, I'll find where they are, I'm sure . . .

I wake up hours later, not knowing how or when I passed out. Yes, yes! Night's here. I can tell: no more light, no more torturous light. Time to go. What time is it? I don't know.

Confusion sets in sometimes. Night removes my sense of time and space. All I know is that I'm going out. My night ritual. It's not harmful. It's my ritual, my time, my way of being free, to be the way I want, no interruptions. The chimes . . . one . . . two . . . three . . . four . . . five . . . six . . . seven . . . eight . . . nine . . . ten . . . eleven . . . twelve . . . just right, just right. Checklist: Rizla, cap, knife; ready. I'm off. Headed out into *my* world. It feels different today. Can't describe it.

Dark, empty street. Dim streetlights provide the only illumination. I stand outside a terraced house looking up at the window. I bring out the photograph, sigh, whimper, cry, howl like a werewolf, then move off to the curses of abusive neighbours who hate having their tranquillity disturbed by my pain. I walk towards Handsworth. A police patrol car tracks past, second-guessing, trying to suss me out. I carry on walking, face straight ahead, peering out the corner of my eye just in case they stop and I have to leg it. They disappear into the gloom.

Alone, I scream at the top of my voice.

'I'm free!'

I stride down the street as if I own it. A confident, asser-tive stride, gladiatorial in stature and size. No one's gonna fuck with me tonight.

Screaming again. 'Did you hear me?'

I stop to roll a spliff. My tongue massages the Rizla, I fondle the soft paper, caress the weed. I remember better days. The days of Studio One and Motown, of James Brown and Earth Wind & Fire, of sound systems and Rasta. Remnants of my past that evaporate like steam. The first pull on the spliff calms me down. I let myself enjoy it, like the sex I used to have.

Tonight it's mild, quite warm I'd say. It feels different somehow, but I can't put my finger on it. You know when you get that gut reaction? I smile. Darkness always makes me smile. This darkness makes me smile even more than usual. I move through the frontline on Lozells Road: urban chaos, car-led drug deals, hustlers, congregating black youths. Devious-looking black men emerging from the shadows while white students hunt for cheap weed or walk by scared and unnoticed. This is real theatre. No pretentious actors here. Everyone is playing a starring role. There's no beginning, middle or end. It just starts somewhere and goes nowhere. The performance is always the same, same outcome. No seats, standing room only. The headache's back. Where's Tom and Jerry? They always desert you when you most need them.

Alleyways are great to walk down. Oh, to be a cat. The danger's past. I can move again. I'm on Holly Road. Big houses. The kind of house I like. It's my mother's house. Too late to go and see her. Ten years too late. Like a snake, I'm shedding my skin. No stars, no moon, just fading streetlights pushing out insignificant beams, the perfect light for a mugger crackhead or gunman, poised, ready to take you out. A sharp pain to my head forces me to the ground. I clasp my head tightly, but the pain drives into me. What the fuck are you looking at? Yeah you, tree. What cat got your tongue? Don't just stand there grinning; help me, you tall piece of shit. Piss off, then! I don't need you. You just stand there trying to look cute. At least I can walk and I ain't as ugly as you. No amount of cream can make your skin smooth.

Sounds of a distant bassline punctuate the air. It sucks me in. Like oral sex, it feels good. I compose myself and head off towards the sounds. Douglas Road . . . kicking blues. Nuff black youths converge. I walk through them. Suspicious eyes glare as I pass. A drug deal goes down. Night people do their business. A woman is being slapped up by her angry man. These are the shadow people. Those who deal, those who sell, those who kill if they have to, bound together by the fear of daylight. Designer clothes wrapped around wasted lives. Surviving, existing, creating fear and misery, preying on the innocent. I am them, they are me; trapped prisoners of our own environment. Black on black, on white, on police, on crack, on bail, on the edge, on the verge of collapse, but who gives a fuck? They don't. It's not about next week, next year. It's about now.

General organized chaos. I move through, hand clasping my knife. A youth steps up to me. Grinning as if he's gonna take liberties with me. He has gold teeth. I hate gold teeth. It was a guy with gold teeth who raped her. He looks just like him. I see rage; there's the sound of blade in neck. He screams. I run off towards Handsworth Park. Panic and screaming, behind me. I don't belong in *their* darkness; I meander in and out of places only I know. I've shaken them off; tomorrow they'll be out seeking revenge. They can't touch me. Tom and Jerry have passed on their knowledge to me. So I've got lots of surprises up my sleeve.

The park provides me with the right camouflage. I'm standing in the centre of the disused bandstand, soaking in the past memories of a bygone era. Brass-band music pours out of the silence. The moment is broken as an eerie, stony silence that sweeps over this space. It becomes darker and colder. I sit on the edge of the bandstand, kicking my feet and imagining water, clear and blue. Caribbean water. Oh, how I remember it. Perched. I hear voices in the wind.

A short distance away a couple have sex. The absence of tenderness, no foreplay, just a good fuck, is that what it's all about? Time to go. I hear approaching anger. No sign of Tom or Jerry.

Rubbish tips! I love rubbish tips. Raw and unspoiled. By day they're ugly, at night they glisten and shine. Dark seas of rubbish and filth, danger lurking behind every plastic bag. People leave you alone here, frightened the smell will disrupt their new perfume or aftershave. I trip over an out-stretched hand and disturb the dying moments of a gang-land hit. Gurgle, twitch and shake. Then it's all over, a small exhalation and a last fight. I close the lids of those scared eyes. I sit and stare at him, wondering if he had children, a mother, anyone who loved him. A soothing blast of Miles Davis wafts through my tired brain. I close my eyes and escape. I'm face to face with myself on a beach in the sun. I'm talking to myself. I look good.

Heavy breathing brings me back. Angry black youths are searching for me. Where to next? Graveyard! They won't find me there. Graveyards don't scare me. They used to but now I can be alone there and no one troubles me. The dead don't worry me; it's the living that are the problem. A new layer of darkness appears and a rat gnaws my ankle. Like Jerry. There's Jerry. Hey, Jerry! I snake around the headstones and pause to catch my breath. Where is that little mouse? We're playing hide and seek.

Headstones seem so final, so bleak to the touch. I run. I run faster than my legs can. I'm running away from them. They're getting closer. I'm tripping and tumbling. I slam into a tree and fall to the ground. I fend off my attackers, cutting one, two, maybe three, until I'm tired.

Feet tired. Legs heavy. Where am I? Something's wrong. This canopy of trees gives me no bearing. A force moves me. I'm being moved. Not in control. A curtain of darkness has descended, blocking my special darkness out. Fragments of previous moments pass me by as if I'm on a speeding train. Ear-shattering bass, the wound in my chest, the waste ground, mortuary slab, school days, first girlfriend. I'm surrounded by feet, but they're walking away. Why are they walking away? I shout. No one answers . . . no one's there

. . . I'm alone . . . lights flicker on and off. Something touches my shoulder. There's *nothing*.

I stand at the water's edge. Sounds. Then silence. I'm cold. I scream and nothing comes out. I gasp and fight for air. Mud . . . sand . . . then water . . . I frantically search for her photograph, but it floats past with all my other memories.

There is light. I hate light but this light smells of sandalwood.

Tom and Jerry smile at me.

A Bowl Full of Silence
Amina Shelly

It was just past four in the afternoon of a very cold January. There was no sun, so no sunset. A thick patch of cloud that had been staring at the ground all day quietly surrendered to darkness. If it were not for the streetlights and the head-lights of the cars that drove past, Shefa wouldn't have been able to see her own nose as she walked home from the shop where she worked selling fabric for saris and salwar kameez. She had almost three hours to kill before her mother expected her home, so she took a walk through Handsworth Park.

Her brother, Shuhel, opened the door, still wearing the blue *longi* that he slept in. She guessed he hadn't brushed his teeth yet – his mouth stank. He spoke as if she was deaf.

'How come you're back so early?' he shot with a six-inch bullet through a giant gun. Shefa ignored her wound. Walked straight into the kitchen. Her mother, Amma, was there, preparing rice for Shuhel, who had to leave for work at half past five. Shuhel worked at an Indian restaurant in Edgbaston. Came home early morning, slept through the day. Her other brother, Shelim, worked in a restaurant in Somerset. He visited home once a week with a black bag of

86

dirty clothes for laundry – that Amma took care of – and a wage much higher than Shuhel's. Shuhel had made sacrifices after Abba, their father, died. He didn't want Amma home alone all day.

Amma, too, was surprised to see Shefa home early but didn't say anything. Shefa grabbed herself a plate. Ate. And with a bowl full of silence went to her room.

Later in the day, the house became half empty. A mother and a daughter left in peace, in harmony, surrounded only by the front door, a back yard, two sidewalls shared with neighbours. A small era of tranquillity. You can take a breath of fresh air. Speak your mind. Speak with yourself or others without interference. Or arguments. Without having to confront two million questions as to why you left your hair loose or occupied the bathroom for too long.

Amma went into Shefa's room. Shefa feigned ignorance of the question marks lilting on Amma's quiet face; mother looked at daughter, pronouncing only her name.

'Shefa!'

Shefa told her how unemployment happened. How she was sick in the mornings and couldn't get to work on time. The management couldn't tolerate it any more. It seemed sensible for her to leave as nicely as she was asked to do so.

Searching for work became a daily task for Shefa. She went everywhere: from post office windows to employment agencies. They advised her to join a training programme, learn office or computing skills to increase her chances of finding a decent job. But Shefa kept declining the offers. She wouldn't even explain why. There was no time for that. Most of the time she tried to escape by avoiding eye contact, speaking with her head down. 'I have other commitments,' she would say. Once she was asked about her marital status. 'I am not married,' she politely replied, 'but my passport is.'

She had no time for training. She needed a job, fast. Earn. Support herself. Most of all, provide proof that she could support her husband. She couldn't let him hang in limbo for too long, waiting for a visa to England. She was not allowed to do that. 'No one is,' said Amma.

Marriage had made its fierce entrance at sixteen. Unstoppable, like river current on a windy day. Someone did try to help – a neighbour from number 64. Shefa called him Chacha-ji. He had intervened, forgetting that he was an outsider.

'The beautiful girl is still too young to be married off,' he suggested.

Shefa wished she could speak with such courage but she never could. Chacha-ji was brave, a friend. She taught him English whenever they met, he needed lessons – had always thought 'guy' meant 'milk-giving cow' because it sounded like *gai* until Shefa corrected him.

Chacha-ji was fond of Shefa, an uncle to her, and watched her grow up from inside a pair of stockings to almost his height. They shared many memories – like the time when Shefa, then only four or five, painted her chin and cheeks in black and grey. Refused to wash it off: if Chacha-ji and she were friends, real friends, then how come he had a beard and she didn't? She liked playing with his beard. Sometimes she insisted on painting the area where his moustache should have been. He never had a moustache.

Shefa was thirteen when Abba and Amma decided that the family should spend the winter in Bangladesh. They said it was important for children to learn as much as possible about their homeland. Chacha-ji came running as soon as he heard the news. 'School is also important for children!' He talked them into postponing the trip till summer.

He tried talking again, before Shefa's wedding. But the harder he tried to put a pause on things the worse the situation became. She couldn't open her mouth in front of Abba. Never did. She only spoke to him when she was spoken to. But Chacha-ji didn't have that problem when her welfare was involved. 'At least let her have a think about it. She still has a year to go in school.'

Then for the first time in years Shefa heard Abba talk at the extreme of his voice. His beard shook, like tiny leafless branches moved by a light winter breeze without the knowledge of the tree. He took his fez down as he spoke and scratched his bald scalp at the end of every sentence.

'She can't think for herself! Children know very little. It's the same with strangers. *We* know what's good for her. Or do you think *you* know better?'

Plain. Simple. And enough to mute Chacha-ji.

Two weeks before they flew to Bangladesh for the wedding, Abba gathered the family over lunch as he did every time he had something important to talk about. He always made Amma cook Shefa's favourite fish *elish*. He called these get-togethers 'family meetings', even though he was the only one who spoke and he decided when they'd finished.

They were all at the table – Amma, Shelim, Shuhel and Shefa. Each just as nervous as the other, except for Shelim. He seemed quite ready for what was coming. Perhaps because he was a grown man. He was as tall as Abba that day.

As they ate, Abba started with his usual speech.

'There's only one Allah. And we only live once. That's why we must finish our earthly duties before we retire.'

He took a two-minute break to concentrate on his food, then continued to speak while the rest of the family ate.

'A father has to do his duty, get his sons and daughters married before he dies. But in my case, it must be the daughter first because you never know what might happen tomorrow. Boys can take care of themselves if need be. But girls . . .

'I have chosen my youngest nephew, Aziz, for Shefa. He's

89

a hard-working fellow. When he comes to the UK it will keep us close to our brothers and bring prosperity to the whole family. We will leave in two weeks' time. If you have anything to say speak now or swallow it with your rice.'

Shefa looked at Amma out of the corners of her eyes. Amma met her daughter's glance, then looked down at her plate, drawing the *aachal* of her sari across her face.

Shefa left everyone eating at the table and took her bowl to her room.

The words of the elders were unquestionable. Especially Abba's words. Especially when he had been ill for several years and kept assuring everyone that he didn't have long to live. He was the guardian of the family after all, and reserved the right to decide what was right for them. Nothing strange about that. There was a person of his stature in every household. What he or she declared important was thought to be true. The way we think of the Quran or the Bible, for example. So Shefa couldn't tell anyone of the boyfriend she dreamed of at night, never mind have a say in her marriage. It was decided and arranged in front of her numbed eyes. A decision, once taken, taken for good. An arrangement declared irreversible.

Shefa had seen her cousin Aziz on her previous trips to Bangladesh – not a dreamboat, but he didn't look bad. He lived in a small village in Sylhet that was home to Abba by birth and to Amma by marriage. It was a wonderful place – if she could have spent the weekend there every now and then – but it could never be somewhere that Shefa wanted to return to at the end of every day. Born in Birmingham, Shefa had a mind that thought of daffodils in spring – unlike Abba, who thought of rice crops. As a child she couldn't work out how a village on the other side of the world could ever become her home. Perhaps Abba had found the answer to that.

Abba had the answer to lots of things, and he always thought his answers the best ones. Whoever nodded their head and agreed with him remained in his good books for a long time. Shefa was in his good books, but only for a short period. One morning, six weeks after Shefa's wedding, Abba forgot to wake up. They called and called him. The sun reached the tin roofs, the shadows changed direction from west to east, but Abba slept on and on until he passed the waking point.

Tired of village life just a month after Abba's burial, Shelim and Shuhel went back to Birmingham. Amma stayed with Shefa, partly to look after her, but mostly because she preferred life in Sylhet. Shefa missed school. She missed her friends – they were preparing for their GCSEs; hers had been replaced with sparkling veils. She wandered around Sylhet, counting the days into weeks, the weeks into months, her husband out in the fields all day and in the market all evening. She'd counted seventeen months by the time Amma decided it was time to pack up.

Aziz had applied for a visa to come to England. But he wouldn't get one until Shefa could prove she earned enough to support her husband and herself in the UK. So Shefa returned to Birmingham with Amma, the luggage and a mission to earn.

At last, a job. A machinist. A seven-months-pregnant machinist at a textile factory. Nine till six was very tiring. Without much hesitation Shefa worked until a baby girl arrived. A small, fragile, beautiful baby girl. They cut her open to bring the child out. Lying on the hospital bed, Shefa pictured her daughter reaching her own height before Shefa turned thirty. Amma suggested all sorts of names for her but Shefa couldn't make her mind up. The child was too beautiful to have an ordinary name. Too beautiful to survive, too fragile to live for longer than a month. This loss was beyond words. Beyond vision.

People kept coming with consolation.

'We know . . .'

'We understand . . .'

No one but Shefa felt the brewing pain. Those who have lost a child understand the loss of a child. But nobody knew the loss of Shefa's child, only Shefa.

But in life there were many other matters to worry about – like a husband in limbo, for one. You have to put your priorities in the right places, and Shefa was no exception. So she composed herself as soon as she could and returned to the machine.

The factory was in Smethwick about five miles from home, the border of Handsworth and Perry Barr. A massive warehouse with a giant table in the centre for cutting materials, surrounded by stacks of cloth. In one corner were sewing machines and a few women, including Shefa, who sat sewing, their tiffins resting by their chairs. Opposite, by the entrance, was a garage – a Toyota van would pick up and drop off employees as well as goods – the toilets, and a small room where the owner and his wife did their office work. Inside, bits of fabric flowed through the air in all directions and the sewing was accompanied by constant sneezing, but worse than this was the bunch of thirsty needles waiting to get hold of hard-working fingers. The needle on Shefa's machine broke at least once a day but she got used to it. She learned to sew more efficiently – still her finger was chosen, for sacrifice perhaps. The needle caught the index finger of her right hand and mangled it so badly that it had to be chopped off down to the end of its nail. It was a long time before Shefa was able to recognize her own hand.

When Shefa came back to Birmingham after her wedding, she'd thought the year she got married was her year of deluge. Then, later, she thought it was the year she had and lost her first child. But the following year, when Aziz finally came to live in England, she was forced to rethink.

Shuhel went back to his old job in Somerset. Amma kept herself busy looking for a girl for Shelim. Shefa quit her job to look after the same old house they all shared. The men were only part-time occupants. Aziz started working in a restaurant in Glasgow immediately after his arrival. He came to see Shefa once a week. Sometimes once every fortnight. People admired many things about him, especially his ambitious attitude, and for this he was forgiven. He was charming, but living together brings bad habits and hidden matters on to the discussion table. On Shefa's, lay an alcoholic, she realized about the same time she discovered she was growing new bones. Was his smoking not bad enough? He needed a chimney over his head every time he moved. But drink? She wasn't sure whether he drank because he liked to or whether it was the lonesome spare time in Glasgow that drove him to it. One day Shefa asked him to find a job near by so that he could be home more.

'I haven't come all this way to stay locked in your doodle case!' he said. He often said that. The rest of his reply was new to her. 'I need to make money. And you'd better get me a boy this time. Make sure he lives, so he can grow up and earn. After all, I can't live here by your mother for ever. Maybe you can, but I can't. I've got home and my brothers to think of.'

Shefa never said a word more.

With the house half empty and all the time in the world in her hands to nurse her wounds, Shefa went to Chacha-ji. He was delighted to see her. He couldn't speak as water filled his eyes. Since he no longer came to their house, Shefa started visiting him and his family quite frequently.

Meanwhile, Amma had found a girl for Shelim. The wedding was set. Everyone was very excited. Chacha-ji didn't come, although Amma invited him. He said it was too cold and that the journey was too long for him. It was February, four winters since Shefa's wedding, three months since her nineteenth birthday and three months before her second child was due.

The bride lived in East London and they went there for the wedding. Waiting for Shefa outside the reception hall was the surprise of her life. It was Chacha-ji, with a winsome face that said he'd hit the jackpot.

'I am sorry I didn't do something earlier, my love.'

He put her in a black cab and told her that she had nothing to fear. Then he handed her a small bunch of keys in an envelope with an address written on it. It was twenty minutes from the reception hall. He told her to keep quiet.

She did.

'. . . and no argument!'

'No!'

And they both smiled.

Shefa settled into the council flat. She gave birth to her second daughter. An angel. She is teething now. Chacha-ji telephones regularly to make sure they are all right.

Shefa misses Birmingham. She misses Amma. She remembers how, when she was a little girl, she wanted to keep a diary of her life and felt sad because she never had much to write about. She has now. Enough to compile a book. But is this what she wanted to write about? Sometimes, when she stands quiet on the balcony of her flat, she remembers her mother's proverb: 'Wherever the main course is rice with fish, dessert is always a bowl full of silence.'

Three Days

Pavan Deep Singh

School holidays were simply great, I remember that everyone looked forward to them, wished they would never end. Well, my memories of school holidays are from the late 1970s, a time which seemed to me always sunny and extremely hot, a rarity in England. Out of all the summers, I remember one when I was ten. The year was 1979.

My English teacher had asked my class to keep a journal over the holidays and to write about all the interesting things that we did. At the time it seemed as if all I would do was play football, relax with my mates and ride my Grifter bike. I mean, being the only child with hardly any cousins or relations living near by meant that nothing interesting was ever going to happen, but boy was I wrong; so very, very wrong.

We were a small family: my mum, my dad and myself. We had a terraced house, 65 Miliners Road, by Victor Park on the outskirts of Birmingham. There was no front garden, the toilet was in the back garden, the living room was the centre of the house. That was where Mum had her sewing machine and anything worth knowing about happened in there. Mum was always busy sewing. A man would come at the beginning of the week in an orange Volkswagen van to drop off lots of stuff for Mum to sew and he would collect the finished pieces the following week. She called it 'piece work'. She started sewing early in the morning and went on until late. She would eat and drink while working on the machine – it seemed as if it never went off – it made an irritating sound, a constant buzzing noise which was really annoying since it made my television viewing extremely difficult.

'Your cousin Jasvir is coming later today from Southall,' Mum said just as I came in from school, ready to watch my weekly dose of *Blue Peter*.

'Jasvir . . . Why is he coming here?' I asked. I had met him once when I went and stayed at his the summer before.

'He's going to marry a girl from Wolverhampton so until then he'll stay with us. After all, your dad and I will be arranging the wedding . . .' Mum rambled on. My dad would say one thing about Mum, that she went on and on, talking nonsense all the time. 'They should be home soon. You'll have a friend to keep you company for a few days over your holidays.'

'But, Mum . . . He's really old, he wears funny clothes and he smells and he's really boring. I don't want him to hang around me and my mates.' As far as I was concerned anyone over twenty was ancient.

'*Nah*. He's only twenty-two and you know he's very clever. I'm sure he'll be a good influence,' Mum stated.

Now, I remember thinking about Jasvir and that he was nicknamed 'Rolly' by everyone because he was a little over-weight – actually, a lot overweight. He was a kind of Jack the Lad, a Del Boy character. He claimed to know every-thing about everyone and all he ever talked about was sex. He had once told me that he went to strip bars regularly and that they were very educational. Of course at the time I didn't know what exactly happened in strip bars.

I was a little concerned – very worried, actually – about the news of Jasvir/Rolly coming to stay with us over the summer and wrecking my holidays. But the news that he was getting married was more than I could handle. I mean the idea of someone actually agreeing to marry him was incredible. It had to be one of those forced marriages that I'd often heard about.

Day One

The first day of my holiday I woke up pretty late – after all, it was only Saturday. I came down wearing my casual T-shirt and shorts and the first person I saw as I stepped into the living room was Jasvir. He was standing in front of the mirror which hung over the fireplace, putting oil on his long hair and flicking it back and forth as he talked to my mum about something or the other. Mum was working and chatting away at the same time. Jasvir always had his hair loose, he wore faded flared jeans, a bright green flowery shirt which was deliberately half-unbuttoned to show off the medallion around his neck. He later told me it was the ultra cool look.

'Say *Sat Sri Akal* to Jasvir,' Mum said.

'Hi,' I mumbled.

'You're very late this morning,' said Mum. 'Your dad went to work ages ago. Why don't you eat something first and then show Jasvir around the local sights? Introduce him to your friends.'

'Yeah right! As if that's going to happen,' I carelessly answered back. Mum didn't look pleased.

'Look, Auntie, don't worry, we're going to become best friends over the next three days,' Jasvir assured Mum. Trying to be cool, I thought, until he followed it up with a huge loud burp.

I looked at him and thought 'how disgusting'. The guy was a slob, an animal. Could I really be related to such a heathen?

'I mean, we're cousins, right! I think we're going to have lots of fun. Come on, move it. Get ready, Cuz, and call me Rolly.' Jasvir spoke with great confidence as he yawned and stretched his arms.

In the end it was decided that we would go for a walk to the park. Despite my objections I had to go. And Jasvir was only going to be around for a few days, so I thought it wouldn't be that bad after all. Then there was the additional emotional blackmail from Mum about losing my Scalextric set if I didn't. We walked out of the house separately: I went first, Jasvir followed. I had given him strict orders to keep his distance from me, but Jasvir, did he listen? No, instead he caught up with me, got out his comb and put it through his hair. I was so embarrassed. What would people think?

The park started at the end of my road and ended, well, somewhere. I was only ten and didn't know everything. I hadn't yet ventured out to see where exactly it ended. But in those days my own road seemed enormous, a world in its own right, even though it had about ten houses and half of them were empty. My road was simple, small, a little derelict and was soon going to be demolished to make way for a new council estate. But it was a quiet cul-de-sac, or a dead end as me and my friends called it. In fact, walking along with Jasvir wasn't really that bad. It was kind of fun listening to his weird stories and especially watching him smoke, holding the cigarette with his third finger – it made him look cool like a gangster. He called it 'a third finger job'.

We seemed to be getting on pretty well and I started to call Jasvir 'Rolly'. I told him almost everything I knew about the neighbourhood – no, actually, I did tell him everything, every little detail, even the things that were supposed to be confidential. Things like who fancied who, who was going out with who, and whose dad was in prison – the usual kind of gossip, but looking back it seems pretty unusual that I knew any of these things at all.

The afternoon was dry, sunny and hot. Abba and Boney M played on the radio constantly. Rolly had bought himself a pocket radio from the corner shop. By today's standards it wasn't small at all and I'm sure that there wasn't a pocket it could really fit into. He kept it switched on and took it with him wherever he went. We spent most of the day walking the wall. The wall was exactly that – a brick wall about six to seven foot high at the back of the back garden. It belonged to the factory which used to be behind the garden until it burned down years before. I was about four or five, maybe six, at the time of the fire. All I remembered was big black smoke clouds, or maybe the big black smoke clouds were in one of my dreams – well, whatever. Ever since then all that remained of the factory was the wall and a big empty space. The wall went along the back of all the ten houses on my road and all the kids would walk across it, throwing stones, swearing, sometimes peeing in people's gardens. It was a kind of dare, to see who was brave enough.

Getting back to Rolly and me. We climbed on to the wall from my garden and sat down. Rolly wasn't exactly cut out to walk the wall; he was out of breath, puffing and panting as soon as he climbed up. I mean, he was too wide and plus he was far too scared. So we just sat on the wall and talked and had what Rolly called 'deep and meaningful discussions'.

As we sat on the wall listening to the radio we talked and looked out at the back of other people's houses and caught a glimpse of what the inhabitants were doing.

'Well, I'll begin at the beginning,' I started. 'Our neighbour, Bibi Bajan Kaur is about sixty.' I pointed her out as she sat in her garden with a tray of lentils. 'She's been married three times, once in India, once in Kenya and once in England and she's rumoured to have at least sixteen kids.'

'Wow, respect man, respect . . .' Rolly was completely shocked – why wouldn't he be? After all, Bibi Bajan looked and behaved like any other old Punjabi lady. She looked religious and everything. Although she was a fan of Jimi Hendrix, which I must admit I always found a bit odd.

'Oh, and whenever a Tarzan movie is on TV, she claims that she can understand the natives, she says she learned the language in Kenya when she lived there, and there's more . . .' I said eagerly. I was letting everything out.

'There's more? Like what?'

'Well, you know Bibi's a Sikh – at least that's what my dad says and she does go to the temple – but she has a weekly visit from a priest, from the church, he's one of those exorcists like in the film. You see she has a ghost living in the house with her, Mum says she thinks it's one of her husbands,' I said in one breath.

'Does she know which one – I mean which husband?' Rolly wondered.

'I . . . I don't know, but I know he stays in the garden shed and he's about six foot three.'

'But that's impossible. The shed's about five foot high, max,' Rolly said, looking towards it.

'Yeah, but he's a ghost. I'm sure he can shape-shift or something.'

'That's heavy stuff. Does Uncle know?' Rolly asked as he tried to digest all the information. 'What about your other neighbours. Are they just as loony?'

'No, I think everyone else is kind of normal. No one in Bibi's league,' I assured Rolly.

'You call that normal?' Rolly was stunned as he pointed to another neighbour's back garden. It was my friend Ranjit's house and his grandma was having a bath on the veranda and she was totally naked for all to see. I gave a reluctant smile but kind of shared Rolly's sentiment that it wasn't a pretty sight nor was it normal to see anyone's grandma naked, having a bath out in the open.

'I think we should do something else, should go from here. If Ranjit finds out we'll end up having a fight,' I said as I fluttered about and got up and climbed down from the wall back into my garden.

Day Two

The day started off with all the kids in the neighbourhood playing 'tig'. I can't remember the rules of the game but it involved a lot of running and chasing. I wanted to play but Rolly wasn't keen. So we sat down on the kerb and watched everyone else play instead.

'Bibi lives next door . . . so who lives the other side?' Rolly asked, trying to make sense of the neighbourhood.

'Well, no one lives on that side at the moment, it's empty. The people who lived there have gone to Glasgow, they've bought a launderette there,' I said, noticing Rolly's eyes light up with excitement. I could tell that he was up to something.

'It's amazing that no one's broken into the house yet,' Rolly said.

'But why would they? I mean, I went in through the back window with Ranjit and a few mates once. There's nothing there. Except it stinks and there's lots of balloons in the garden shed.' Rolly didn't reply, but just looked at me as if I was stupid or something.

'Let's go and take a look,' said Rolly quickly as he got up and walked away towards the house.

'I know how to get in through the kitchen window,' I said as I followed.

'No, I don't want to go in the house, but the shed. Let's

101

see what's in there,' Rolly said as he walked through the entry to the back.

I climbed over the fence from my back garden; it was easier for me. Rolly waited for me to open the gate to let him in. Once in the garden we walked up to the house. It was exactly the same as mine but in much worse condition. The toilet was in the back garden and had been trashed; the windows were all boarded up. Rolly wasn't very interested in the house so he moved to the back towards the shed and I followed him.

The shed walls were made up of old doors with some corrugated iron sheets as the roof. It was a kind of blue-green colour and the paint was crumbling off. Then we discovered that the door to let us in was padlocked.

'I thought you'd been in the shed,' Rolly remarked.

'Yeah . . .' I stuttered.

'Well, it's locked. Who uses this place anyway?' Rolly asked impatiently.

'The older kids from the top of the road. I think it's their den. It's not a very good lock,' I said as I picked up a stone and broke the lock open. 'Look, there, I told you.'

'But now they're going to know that someone has broken in,' said Rolly frantically.

'Yeah. But they're not going to find out who and, besides, it happens all the time. They'll just get a new lock,' I assured Rolly.

We walked into the shed and looked around. It was dark and smelled funny. There was a huge old mattress on the floor. Rolly snooped around and found some magazines hidden under the mattress. When I caught a glimpse of them I noticed they were no ordinary magazines, they had women with no clothes, no underwear, you could see everything. I mean everything. Rolly was flicking through the pages with great interest.

'This shed's a . . .' He laughed out loud. Rolly found an

old bottle of gin hidden in a broken cabinet by the mattress and took a few sips.

'So these older kids . . . Who are they?' Rolly asked as he sat on the mattress.

'Just some guys and girls.' I replied innocently.

'What? Girls as well?' Rolly said, somewhat bemused.

'Yeah.'

'When do they come?' Rolly persisted.

'Every day in the evening about five,' I said.

'OK, put those magazines under the mattress, we'll come back later.' Rolly checked the time on his watch and put the gin back where he found it.

'Can I take the magazine?' I asked. I wasn't sure why but I wanted to take the magazine and show it to my friends.

'No,' came the sudden and abrupt reply. And that was that.

Later that day we watched and we watched from my garden, peeking through a small hole in the fence. We waited until we heard noises from next door's shed.

'Looks like someone's there,' Rolly said after some time. 'Bingo! I think they're inside.'

I jumped over the fence like I had earlier and let Rolly in through the gate in the entry. We walked to the shed and stood outside. Rolly put his head against the shed wall and listened to the giggling, chattering and whispering that went on inside. He then scouted around and found a few crates which he lined up on top of each other, climbing up and peering through the cracks in the top of the wall. I whispered loudly to Rolly, since I wanted to climb up and see what was going on as well. But before I could, a huge thud and crashing sound overcame me: it was Rolly! He had fallen into the shed. Then there was a great deal of swearing in both English and Punjabi, and half-dressed people running out of the shed.

Day Three

The day was just as hot and again we were on the wall looking down at the houses. Rolly had his radio on and was chewing gum, while I sat with my milkshake in my hand.

'Who lives next door to Bibi?' Rolly asked curiously as he smoked his cigarette.

'Aunties. There's three of them. Oh, and there's an uncle who comes around there a lot,' I said. Back in those days I called everyone either uncle or auntie. At times it was difficult to keep track of all the uncles and aunts.

'Do you ever go there?' Rolly persisted.

'Yeah, sometimes. Especially when our football goes into their garden. The aunties are really nice, but the uncle . . . well, I don't like him at all,' I said. Mum didn't like any of the aunties and used to cuss them in Punjabi all the time.

'Have you got some money?' Rolly asked, checking his wallet. 'Oh, it's OK, I've plenty. Let's go and say hi to them.' He plunged off the wall and headed through the garden for the entry to the front.

'Why now?' I shouted. But as I got to the front he'd already passed Bibi's house and was standing outside the aunties' house.

'Well, hurry up. Aren't you coming?' Rolly called out.

I quickly caught up with him. As soon as I got to the house I knocked on the door. Both Rolly and I waited in anticipation for someone to open it. Finally, after a few seconds, the door opened.

'Hello. Have you lost something?' asked the voice. It was one of the aunties, the tall blonde one with big jugs, and what a sexy voice she had.

'Erm . . . No . . . We just came round,' I said, catching my breath. My voice squeaked and my legs trembled.

'Yeah . . . Hi. Just being neighbourly,' Rolly said with great conviction. He shrugged his shoulders and pulled up his shirt collar and began to flick his comb through his hair.

'Oh, well, you boys better come in and meet the rest of the girls then,' the woman said as she began to bop her head along to the Tom Jones song playing inside.

'I like the sound of that,' said Rolly as we stepped inside.

'By the way, my name is Stella. Meet Ruby and Sheila,' she said, pointing at two other women sitting on the couch. She leaned down to the coffee table, picked up her cigarette and lit it. Ruby and Sheila were humming *Delilah, Delilah* as they sipped their drinks.

I remember thinking that the aunties were very different – well, weird, totally unlike any of the other aunties in the neighbourhood. They were a bit wild: listening to loud music, drinking, smoking and dancing around their house. To make matters more confusing for me, there wasn't even a sewing machine in their living room. It was hard for me to imagine how they earned a living. All I could think was that maybe the uncle who came round once in a while must have been really rich – he did have a brand-new Cortina. Well, whatever, they sure did seem to have fun, maybe that's why no one liked them. But Rolly seemed to be quite comfortable in the living room. Thinking about it, I guess most men were.

'The boys have come round to see us,' said Stella.

'Great! That should be fun,' said Ruby sarcastically. 'Why don't you show them around the house?'

'Come on,' said Stella as she encouraged Rolly to follow her into the back room. I got up to go with them. 'No, I think you should stay there for a while.' So I stayed there with Ruby and Sheila, both of them getting plastered. I waited and waited for Rolly and Stella to come back into the front room, and then after about fifteen minutes Rolly strolled in smirking and patting his belly, something he did

105

when he was very happy. Whatever happened in the back room, Rolly was very happy.

After that I went home alone and Rolly stayed. He spent the rest of the day with the aunties. I didn't quite understand at the time why he'd told me not to tell my mum or dad. But he did say that the aunties were helping him. Judging by the amount of time he spent there they certainly seemed to help quite a bit.

'Where's Rolly?' asked Mum as I sat bored, watching television. 'Where's he gone on his own leaving you here? It's getting late.'

'He's found some new friends that's all,' I said cautiously.

'Friends . . . So he can still take you with him. Have you two had a fight?' Mum asked.

'No. It's just that his friends aren't my type,' I said, kind of knowing what Mum would ask next.

'Who are these friends? Do they live around here?'

'Yeah, two doors down, next to Bibi's. He's gone to see the aunties. He says that they're helping him,' I blurted out. I knew that Mum would be furious and that Rolly would be in serious trouble. But I kind of secretly wanted to get Rolly in trouble. I wasn't sure why but I did.

There was a minute's silence, followed by Mum switching off her sewing machine. That was the first and last time I had ever seen Mum switch the machine off during the day. And then she started hurling abuse in Punjabi at the aunties and at Rolly. She got up from her chair, grabbed her shawl, wrapped it around her and stormed out of the house. She walked down the road shouting and swearing until she reached the aunties' house. She then shouted and swore louder and more vigorously until one of the aunties opened the door. I watched from our front door until Mum went in. By then most of the other neighbours had gathered round to see what the fuss was all about and I no longer had such a good view. A few minutes later Mum came out with Rolly. She dragged him along the street, swearing, shouting and hitting him on the head with one of her slippers.

After that I didn't get a chance to speak to Rolly much. Later that day when my dad came back from work, Mum and Dad spent hours talking about what had happened. The next day Dad took Rolly back to Southall, just as he had brought him to Birmingham a few days before.

Well, those few days were certainly interesting. And because of them it was the best summer holidays I ever had. After that summer nothing was really the same again: the sun never shone so brightly and Abba were no longer in the charts; Blondie and Adam and the Ants had taken over. It was a changing time, the punk era had arrived and everything seemed different.

Covenant

Leone Ross

Have you turned the tape recorder on? Maybe you should let me collect my thoughts first. This might be one of your harder debriefing sessions. I'm not saying I don't want to tell you; this sharing process is one of the reasons I came to the Covenant. I liked the idea of sharing in this way. I think it brings us all closer together. But I don't know where to start. I've been here for a couple of weeks and I knew this interview was coming. Your literature says it is part of the process, but I still feel unprepared. But I am so pleased with my entry presentation. I think it was a good choice.

I guess it would be best to start at the beginning. You will tell me if I go off track, won't you?

It was easy to leave Abe in the end, after turning it over so many times in my mind. I wasn't happy. I wanted more. I did try – for nearly twenty years. Straight out of my father's house into Abe's arms.

I haven't thought about my father for a while. Mornings like this, they make me think of home. So clear and silent. I'd wake Daddy up so he could get me ready for school. All the men in my life sleep hard. Abe sleeps like the dead. I've set out his clothes for a business meeting, I've read books with my bedside lamp blaring in his face, I've walked up and down the bedroom with Isaac teething and wailing, and that man kept right on itching, fidgeting, farting and sleeping. About a month ago I lay beside him and stuck him with a pin. A sharp one, it slid in like butter. I tried different parts of his body, near to the bone, through his belly, deeper each time. He flapped at me like I was a mosquito. Didn't open his eyes. I did it for ten minutes. He was covered with tiny pools of blood. I sat there and I thought, boy, you could sleep for Jamaica.

I didn't do a lot of sleeping in those last months. I went for long walks at night. The darkness meant I didn't have to pretend I was OK. Two o'clock in the morning, the dark made the bruises on my hands fade away. I walked towards the high street and ran down the middle of the road until I was panting, until my legs were trembling. It was so quiet, only the noise of cars in the distance. I stopped in front of people's houses and pretended I could hear them breathing. I wondered if they were lying warm in their beds and in their perfect existences.

Mamma painted my room pink before she left, that's what my father told me. I was three. After she'd gone there were screaming pink sheets, an army of Barbies and a birthday party every year. Bouncy castles and bags of sweeties. Balloons and heart-shaped plastic earrings. Bottles of perfume, a silvery little choker, a golden diary with a matching pen, high-heeled shoes. All the boys had to come into the front room and sit on the mahogany sofa and state their intentions. Now I have pink nails. I saw you looking at them when I arrived. Everybody does. They don't fit, do they? Look, I've broken three already.

Abe didn't like broken nails. It was all that hand to hand combat. Then he'd make me an appointment with my manicurist. 'Ten thirty,' he'd say. 'Sarah, can you make it?'

When I was eight, me and Mary-Anne Gervan snapped the heads off all my Barbies. I think we wanted to see what was inside. We cut off their hair and laid them out in a row on the bed, admiring them. My father came in and started to shout, *You know how much dem tings cost?* Boy, him cuss, him cuss, him cuss Mary-Anne. He told her mother that she couldn't play with me any more. Then he took me on his lap and hushed me. I was happy that I wasn't in trouble, but I wanted to cry. I liked Mary-Anne. When he put me to bed I couldn't sleep. I kept seeing her big brown eyes fill with tears. I got out of bed and went into the front room where he was drinking beer and I told him. I was scared that he would shout at me, but I knew it wasn't fair.

Daddy told me that lying wasn't nice and that I should never lie, not even for my friends. He said he knew his little girl wouldn't ever break the dolls he'd bought her. Then he turned back to the TV and the beer and told me to go to bed. I fell asleep, looking at the doll hair in the wastepaper basket. Golden curls.

Sorry, I'm rambling. Is this the kind of detail you want to hear?

Leaving . . . yes, leaving. I told you, it was simple. I went into Isaac's room and I stood there for a bit, looking at the yellow moons and the silver stars on his bedroom ceiling. Abe painted them with a special fluorescent paint that twinkles in the dark. I guess he was trying to remind his son of home. He painted waves around the edge of the walls. That was kind. He could be kind.

I woke Isaac up. He rolled over and looked at me with his face full of sleep. Deep eyes like wet river stones. Poor baby. He let me dress him, not a whimper. His cheek was warm against my face, leaning against me, still in dreamtime. Like his father. He asked me, 'Mamma, whatcha doin'?' and I said, 'We're going on an adventure, baby. You want to go on an adventure with Mamma?' And he nodded his head, and his face was all speckled with those moons and suns.

He went back to sleep in the car. I was worried that he'd roll off the seat when I reversed, but he didn't. He lay there, sucking his thumb. Abe doesn't like the suck-thumb business. He used to slap Isaac's wrist, not hard, but slapping anyway. Told me that if we were still in Jamaica he would get aloe vera and smear it on Isaac's fingers. You ever seen fresh aloe vera? No, I guess you haven't. Anyway, it tastes metallic, really bad. Abe said it would break the habit, that his mother used to do it to him.

A couple of hours later I was feeling fine, driving round the M42 thinking that leaving at night isn't so scary, especially when you're heading towards freedom. The road was bright with lights and I have to thank you people – you signposted well. Every few miles that little red arrow and THE COVENANT. I appreciated the support, how you knew I'd be coming a long way, at night and with a child. When you told me on the phone that you'd booked us into a hotel, I was really pleased. I felt like crying when you told me that. Did you know I was getting choked up? You didn't, did you? I'm very good at hiding my feelings. It's been essential.

Cars passed us sometimes, covering us with quick beams. My hands had stopped shaking and I was desperate for a smoke, but it was too cold to crack a window and I didn't want to fill the car with fumes and disturb Isaac. It was the best way to wake him, lighting up in his room. He'd wriggle, open his eyes and frown and look at me and say, 'Mamma, you smokin'!' I'd hide the cigarette behind me and he'd sit up and chase the grey fumes through the air, laughing.

My father didn't believe that little girls should run. Or sweat. So I joined the track team. My father didn't believe that little girls should smell bad, so I didn't brush my teeth for days. I stank through half of third form until the Personal

Development Programme teacher took me into the nurse's office and pressed a gift pack on me. Deodorant and soap and body spray and toothpaste, wrapped in ribbon. I went into the school bathroom afterwards and rubbed my sanitary pad on the walls. The streaks went brown across the graffiti. Obliterated all the Susanne-heart-Bobbies and the I-love-Adrians.

We got to the Holiday Inn and the receptionist lowered her voice when she saw Isaac snoring in my arms. She buzzed a boy to take the luggage and in the elevator we watched the lights on the panel run up and down: first, second, third, fourth floor. I was near to dropping when we got to our room. The boy helped me put Isaac on the bed and we stood there and watched him snuffle, dead to the world, spit leaking out of the side of his mouth on to the pillow.

The bag boy grinned and told me he was a lovely lad, then he got all embarrassed. He was tripping over his shoes and trousers that looked two sizes too big for him. 'He looks like you,' he told me, heading out the door. Everybody says that. It's funny how everybody says that.

Do you know that poem, the one that talks about what happens when a dream is deferred? It's by a black poet; maybe you wouldn't recognize it. When I was fourteen I scribbled down a version of it. I think I can still remember.

> *My dreams are always deferred*
> *put off*
> *kept waiting*
> *thwarted*
> *stopped*
> *jilted*
> *flung away*
> *trodden on*

> *coaxed into oblivion*
> *my dreams are always*
> *noted*
> *filed for reference*
> *and fantasy*
> *my dreams are always deferred.*

Melodramatic, but not bad for a fourteen-year-old. And I'm sure you can relate.

Having Isaac was Abe's idea, but I was desperate enough to agree. I was a wife and I needed a child. Especially before we came here. The women in Jamaica were already asking me what happen, you and Abe not having pickney, something wrong with you? *Normal, normal, normal,* I kept thinking. Give it up, Sarah, give up the fantasies and deal with reality. Being who I really was, ah, it felt too hard. Easier to be a good little girl. The punches and the screams were less complicated. Hagar was less complicated. She sat there in my living room, wiggling her dirty toes and sticking out those perfect, nineteen-year-old breasts. You know the perky ones that don't need a bra? I never had breasts like that. We told her that there was nothing wrong with Abe's sperm, just me: barren, empty, the problem. Abe was trying to go on like it was a small thing while he was talking; I guess he was trying to make me feel better. But it was a big thing. And when we were done, the bitch sat there, wiggling her toes, looking confused.

'So . . . Missa Abe, me an' you . . .?' she said.

I could have killed her for saying it, but I looked at her toes and she looked at her toes. They were bright fuchsia pink. I thought that it was like the fuchsia on my nightstand and why the hell did she think she had a right to pink toenails, anyway? She wore it better than I did.

Abe laughed. He was like a pickney in a toy store. He put a hand on her shoulder. I stood there thinking, *You should be touching my shoulder, I'm the one who needs it*. I watched that hand and I wondered how it would change if he gained weight or if he lost weight or how it would look after years of a cold climate, and what did the bones look like underneath.

And he said, 'No, no, Hagar. Not at all like that. I'll provide you with the um . . . sperm . . .'

She didn't say anything but there was a smile on the end of her face. Abe tried again: 'You know, Hagar. I will . . . um . . . get some of my sperm and give it to you, and what you need to do is . . .' Then he looked at me. *Woman's business*, I could hear him thinking.

So I said, 'Hagar, what me and Mr Abe want you to do is take some of his spirit, you know, spirit? And put it inside your body, in your privates. It has to be at a special time. When do you see your monthlies?'

She giggled. The little bitch giggled, with her bleeding, fertile self.

Still, maybe I'm not being fair to her. She was only a country girl, and ignorant. I was getting ready to feel sorry for her when she looked up straight into my husband's face. There was a blazing sun in each eye.

'I can only do it God way,' she said. We stared at her. I don't think Abe knew what she meant right away, but I did. 'If you want it, me have to do it . . . God way.'

Abe is a handsome man, but she never had to make it so obvious. Even now, he's a mile of striated muscles and the grey looks good on him. I stood still. I couldn't believe we were all there on this normal day, discussing my man fucking this woman. And it's running through my brain. *She wants him. She wants to tie him to her with her tight body*. He looked at me. I gritted my teeth and told him I'd think about it.

I sat on that hotel bed that night and wondered about coming here and about what it would feel like to do everything I wanted to do, what it would be like to finally move past the compromises. I was used to holding back, trying to be what the world says is normal. But normal isn't the same for everybody.

I started to grin, then chuckle, and then I was muffling the sound of my laughter in the pillow so I wouldn't wake up my boy. I lay there with my whole body shaking and I was so . . . joyous. So thankful for the Covenant. So thankful for you and the morning you came to my house, like an inside-out Jehovah's Witness. It felt so good. You get so isolated. I never knew I'd meet another woman who felt the same way I did. You put it all out there: that I had to be sure, that I'd never be able to go back. I was drunk with happiness. It's not a dream deferred that's hard to accept. We all expect failure. It's a dream realized that plays with your head at night, that tempts you and asks you if you dare reach out and take it. You told me that I was special and no one ever told me that before. No one ever told me that, but I felt it.

When I was a little girl, I pulled the wings off butterflies and took them to show my father. I told him that I pulled the wings off the butterflies: *me, Daddy, me, me*. But he said that maybe some kinds of butterflies shed their wings before they die and he went and looked in the encyclopaedia. When he couldn't find the reference he wanted to fit into his pastel pink world he patted me on the head and told me not to cry. I stood there and I yelled into his face, *I'm NOT crying*.

I told him that I'd hated my first-form teacher because she picked boogers out of her nose and wiped them on her shirt. And I told him that I didn't like the girl who sat next to me in class all through fourth form because she was ugly. And I told him that sometimes when I go on those nice dates with those nice boys, Daddy, I want them to lift up my shirt and suck on my nipples, yes, I do, I do. But he just sat there, with this grin on his face, saying that I was so sweet, so beautiful, Daddy's best girl, Mamma would be proud of me if she was here, and I started wondering if he really could hear me. Perhaps I was opening my mouth and no sounds were coming out.

I went off into the back yard afterwards and followed red ants through the dust, around the mango trees, watching them carry leaves like a tiny army. They looked like a trail of blood through the yard. That was a good morning. I picked them up and popped them between my finger and thumb and sniffed the mush on my hands. One bit me: I can still see its jaws opening and crunching down. I howled. It hurt like hell, but I was happy. At least the ant saw me. Felt me. Acknowledged the danger before I crushed it into obscurity.

I didn't know it then, but now that I think about it, things started to change the night my husband had sex with the maid. He was gone for two hours. One hundred and twenty minutes of my life. For the first fifteen I couldn't get the pictures out of my head. I imagined him using the tricks he used on me. The way he kissed my lips, gently, and that look in his eyes, so thirsty, when I took off my clothes in front of him. The way he brought the palms of his hands up, around my sides, leaving the cupping of my breasts until the very last minute.

When he came back he kissed me and I bit a chunk out of his tongue. He sat on the floor with blood coming out of his mouth. I stepped on his right hand and twisted my high heel. I kicked him in the face. I grabbed his testicles and squeezed. He grunted softly and tears poured down his face. And his eyes, oh, they were different, yes, that was it. It wasn't a frozen moment; it was only a tiny shift. But I knew and I stopped because it didn't *sweet* me any more. I sat on the floor next to him and cried.

It was never the same after that; I really see that now. But I kept on beating him. That was our way. I broke his jaw with a rolling pin when he was late home for the dinner I made especially for his boss. I poured Isaac's hot oats across his bare arms at breakfast. But his eyes kept changing. There was a kind of peace there. A kind of contentment.

My fantasies didn't stop. They just got . . . technicolour. I tried to get a little bit of joy. In the supermarket a baby was crying too damned much and I put my nails down his plump back and watched his stupid mother's face crumpling when she heard his wail rise a notch. I drove down the street and ran my wheels across a dog's back, got out of the car, ran up to the owner splayed out on his knees in front of his dog's juddering, dying body: *oh my God, I am so sorry, I didn't see it in time*. I found a dead bird full of dancing maggots in my neighbour's garden, her drinking cold Tango, me turning back to her – *oh dear, don't look* – but she had to and I pulled her hand away from her face – *calm down, take deep breaths, horrible, isn't it, look at me, don't look at it, are you all right now?* Then you arrived like a jack-in-the-box on my doorstep. I didn't want to open the door – I was watching old horror movies, winding, rewinding on faces, jagged, broken open, distended cheekbones, pupils dilating, brown ones and green ones and blue ones. But you went right on knocking. How did you know?

I didn't think it would be so pretty here. It looks like a summer cottage for rich people. The morning we came here, well, I felt like I was coming home. It was raining but we didn't care. Me and Isaac parked and then walked up the trail. He was holding my hand and skipping. I had to trot to keep up with him. The air was fresh and I thought, *I've done it, I've done it*. Isaac said, 'Mamma, we drove hundreds and thousands and trillions of miles!' and I said, 'Hundreds and thousands and trillions,' and he said, 'Like through space in a time ship!' and I laughed and said, 'Yes, like through time in a space ship!' And he said, 'Mamma, you smilin!' He looked at me for a minute like it was a miracle.

Then he let go of my hand and ran through the rain up to
the gate. He was like a jewel under the clouds; I could see
that underneath his baby fat there was this whole promise
of change: cheekbones, biceps, height, hair on his chest and
arms and in between his legs. And I thought it would be
majestic to watch but it would take too long.

Isaac ran up to Brian immediately. I'm not surprised he chose
Brian from all the men here. Brian is good with children and
Isaac must have known that; he was tending the big fire out
back, I could smell the sweet meat on the barbecue and I realized I was hungry. Isaac stared at the fire. 'Yay, fire!' he said.

'Yay, fire!' I said, too. Brian knew our names; I really liked
that. Isaac was hopping up and down on one foot. He asked
Brian whose fire it was and Brian told him it was everyone's fire. Isaac, well, you know how kids are, he said, could
it be *his* fire. Brian smiled at him and said of course it could
be his fire.

I set my 'sweet sixteen' birthday on fire. I watched parents
grab their kids as the tablecloth went up and the pretty
candles melted and sweltered in the heat. I broke the ankle
chain off me – Daddy's present to me on my fifteenth
birthday – and put my fist through the cake.

I didn't know I was crying until you came up to me and
wiped my face.

Daddy gave me a kitten after he'd cleared away the black
cake and the shocked kids. It was grey with a little white
moustache and silver socks. Daddy insisted that I sleep with
it in my bed. He took a picture of it in my arms after he'd
put a bell on the baby blue collar around its neck. I liked the
kitten. I liked the sounds it made. I think I was getting tired
of the fight to get my father to see *me*, not this idea in his
head. If it wasn't for that kitten I'd be a good little girl today.
Pink nails, high heels, all pretty with my husband.

When I woke up the kitten was warm, but very still. It was an accident, I swear. A wonderful accident. I tiptoed into the garden and hid it by the back gate, feeling how heavy and floppy it was.

Two days later I went back to see the body. I put a finger on the fur and jumped. It was hard, like rocks. Its belly was swollen and its tongue was black. I sat on my heels and tried to remember what it felt like when it was alive. I pressed a finger into the belly. It made a *ssss* sound and there was a bad smell. Once it was alive and now it was dead. I was so excited. Did you feel that way the first time? Sure you did, yes, makes you laugh to remember, doesn't it? Remember when we were innocent?

Women bring style to the task. We make it personal. You said my entry presentation was a nice touch. Who did you do? Your boss? That's hilarious. What was he like? Big condescending asshole, huh? Yes, I know the type. Walking around you in the office, not seeing who you are, or your power, not seeing all you could do. You mean you carted him all the way down here? Wait, I know how you did it: sex, right? He thought he was having an affair. What did you use? A candelabra? That's so funny. Hysterical. Did it take a long time?

Your brochures talk about women: *History has shown a domestic tendency in women. Female members should make all necessary efforts to take their projects out of the home. The craft is more than a cottage industry.* That made me really nervous, I admit. I worried that my entry presentation wasn't going to be enough, and I'd come all this way. I felt like an amateur. But you made me feel better, you gave me confidence. You told me the domestic approach was fine for entry level, but I'd have to look elsewhere quickly. You don't have kids, do you? No. So I guess you didn't have the option. Would you have taken it? No? Wow. So, I'm the first?

Leone Ross

Yesterday I heard Brian humming a song Isaac had taught him. Remember them singing together that first day? Isaac was singing loud in his baby voice, a gorgeous voice, and Brian was trailing along behind.

'Father Abr'am had many sons . . .'

'. . . had many sons . . .'

'And many sons had Father Abr'am . . .'

'. . . Father Abraham . . .'

'And I am one of them, and so are you . . .'

'. . . so are you . . .'

'So let's jus' praise the Lord, right han', left han' . . .'

'Right foot, left foot . . .'

I remember what I thought before I began my presentation. I thought of the kitten blowing up, then shrinking, flesh to bones, the sinew toughening and the fur flaking to the earth, the bones turning the colour of urine, then black, then dust. I thought of my father's face when he found me with it, the honest horror, the slow realization that filled his eyes as he looked down at the guts on my hands and my face. I was so happy I tried to hug him. I mean, finally. He saw me, he saw me.

I wanted to use my hands. There is joy in that. Flesh on flesh. It was beautiful. I leaned down to him, close as a whisper. And he said, 'Whatcha doin, Mamma?' and I said, 'This is the adventure, baby,' and the fear in his eyes filled the whole world.

I went up to look at him yesterday. He's under the moon and the stars. Getting on nicely. He's still swelling. I think about it at night; his body swelling, undulating. Crumbling and darkening. I'm going to put him on the fire when he's bones.

He'll smell like dreams.

Invisible Woman

Tonya Joy Bolton

On a freezing day in February, I left Wolverhampton University with my friend Helen. We'd had an intense evening lecture and caught the bus back home to Birmingham.

'I don't know how we're expected to write three thousand words by Thursday,' Helen complained, reapplying her scarlet lipstick. 'I didn't grasp a word of that lecture.' She sighed. 'Oh well, as long as I scrape a pass I'm not bothered.' Her usual couldn't-care-less attitude. 'How do you cope with it all, Ebony? Running your own flat, work and uni? You always manage to get straight As. What's your secret?'

'I cope because I have to and it's bloody hard.' I yawned. 'I don't know how long I can do this for; I'm falling asleep at work and in lectures. Did you see Tony Blair on the news last night spouting on about how he supports students? The joker makes me sick, man.'

'Yeah, I guess I'm lucky I don't have to work,' said Helen. 'I mean, my parents pay my rent and Daddy's buying me a car next month to make travelling easier.'

'Well, I guess it's all right for some,' I teased.

As we chatted about how tough our last year at uni was

and the pressure of dissertation deadlines, a teenage boy carrying a large bottle of beer boarded the bus. He opened all the windows on his way up the bus, sat down a few rows in front of us and lit a cigarette. Irritated, I couldn't decide which was worse – the icy chill that engulfed the bus or the stale stench of his sweat, alcohol and cigarette smoke blowing in my face. He guzzled down his beer and threw the empty bottle down the bus. Like all the other passengers I said nothing, hoping that if I ignored him he would soon disappear along with his foul smell.

As the bus sped down the Wolverhampton Road, I felt numb with cold. Helen and I carried on chatting and for a few minutes I forgot he was there. Then, out of the corner of my eye, I saw him spit – over and over again, aggressively, wanting to be noticed – aiming his spittle across the other side of the bus. Helen and I looked on in disgust as the yellow slime rose high in the air like a flying slug, then slid down the window like ectoplasm. I felt sick and clasped my hand over my mouth to stop myself from heaving. I looked at Helen and she looked at me. Both of us were shocked and appalled by his behaviour but, unable to contain ourselves, we burst out laughing at this salivating animal.

It was then that he swung his puny, pale, chicken-like head around and addressed me.

'You got something to say, you fucking ugly black cunt? You're *nothing*, man, I'll fucking batter you.'

His words slapped me in the face, one by one, burning like acid. I immediately stopped laughing. The chitter-chatter that had previously buzzed around the bus died away. Everyone awaited my reaction. I was frozen.

He glared at me, hatred shooting from his eyes, but I stared back, daring him to attempt anything. I was Medusa, killing him with one look. How dare he disrespect me? I wanted to knock him out with one almighty blow and yell, 'Come on then, you racist tosser!' I couldn't find any other words to express my anger.

It was my friend who spoke, reminding me that she was still there.

'Shut up, you sad racist,' Helen said.

He turned around again and addressed only me. 'Didn't I warn you? Nigger! Bitch! Freak!' He paid no attention to my pretty white friend.

'It wasn't her. It was me!' Helen shouted. 'So what are you going to do about it?'

He stayed silent and carried on demonically spitting his phlegm at the walls. Although I was appreciative of Helen's support, I was painfully aware of the differences that stood between us as women, the unequal positions of power we occupied in the external world. I am black. She is white. He had said nothing to her, yet everything to me. He had no issues with her, but saw me as an inferior colour and because of that he viewed me not as a woman but mere female anatomy and nothing more.

I looked around the bus and saw only blank faces. They averted their stares and said nothing. My frustration began to overtake me and I prayed to God for strength. I no longer felt the cold as my hands trembled in anger, waiting for permission to defend me. I jammed my jaw shut, clenching my teeth tightly together as my warrior spirit tried to escape and assert itself. I didn't want to be condemned by others to the same category as this ignorant fool. I felt powerless. Hiding my humiliation, I laughed and chatted with Helen once again. But my head was filled with the knowledge that he had offended both my race and gender. Had I been white, he could not have referred to me as 'nigger'. Had I been a man, he could not have called me 'cunt' or 'bitch'.

*

An hour later as the bus pulled into Broad Street, I reassured Helen that I'd be perfectly safe and she got off near her apartment. I wasn't going to let him get to me. I sat back in my seat, pleased with myself for keeping silent – the power and victory remained mine. I was proud of myself, and thanked God for my growth and development.

When the bus finally approached my city-centre stop I jumped up, eager to get home. As I walked past him he knocked me to the floor. While I was struggling to get back on my feet he blocked my way. I scanned the bus for help, but we were alone together on the top deck.

I screamed, hoping that someone would hear me, but the bus kept on going.

'If I were you, I wouldn't keep making that racket,' he snarled, waving his finger in my face. 'Looks like it's just you and me. No one's 'ere to fight your battles now.'

I got to my feet and tried to run towards the stairs but he was in front of me. 'Me dad always says you animals have forgotten your place and need to be taught a lesson.'

'You need to get real. This is the twenty-first century,' I said, suddenly conscious that I felt more pity than fear for this pathetic psycho.

'I don't friggin care what century we're in. You coloureds don't belong here,' he ranted.

'Oh please. I've just as much right to be here as you. At least I can string a sentence together,' I snapped. 'And who are you calling coloured? After all, it's not me who's got a face like a beetroot!' I sniggered, remembering the poem my mother taught me when I was a child:

> *When I was born, I was black,*
> *And when I'm embarrassed, cold, or dead,*
> *I am still black,*
> *But when you are born, you are pink,*

When embarrassed, you turn red.
When cold, you go blue, and green when dead.
Yet you have the nerve to call me coloured!

'I'm gonna wipe that fucking smile off your face!' he threatened, moving closer towards me. I knew I was in real danger, so I backed away and yelled at the top of my voice. Almost immediately the bus stopped and a policeman came marching up the stairs. I couldn't believe it.

'You all right, love?'

I nodded, catching my breath.

'Right, so what's happened here then?' the policeman demanded.

'He attacked me!' I said. 'I was just about to get off –'

'She's lying,' the youth interrupted. 'I was just getting off and she tried to trip me up. Stuck her foot right out!'

'What!' I laughed. 'I don't think so. That's absolute crap. If you believe that, you'll believe anything. He was calling me names and making racist remarks.'

The policeman patted me on the shoulder as if I was his pet dog. 'Now, calm down, love. Obviously there's been a misunderstanding. I'm sure we can sort this out,' he said patronizingly. I stood there in disbelief. He was ignoring me as though I were a silly little girl with a chip on her shoulder.

'So what started this?' he asked, still addressing the youth. He folded his arms across his protruding beer belly and rocked back on his heels. It was obvious that this policeman was far more interested in looking important than doing his job. I didn't exist.

'Hello!' I shouted, looking him in the eye. 'I've just told you; this youth has assaulted me racially and physically.'

'Please, miss, I told you to calm down,' he ordered, try-ing to stare me out. His condescending tone was more than I could bear.

'Calm down? I've told you twice that this guy's just attacked me and you call it a misunderstanding?'

The policeman sighed. 'Look, let's just sit down and try to sort –'

'No way,' I interrupted. 'Your sort always sticks together. I'm going to have this man done for assault. This matter is far from over, but this conversation is. I've got your badge number. You'll be hearing from my solicitor. You obviously don't know how to do your job, but perhaps the courts will show you.' I looked the red-faced youth up and down, infuriated by his smugness. He said nothing and showed no remorse as the policeman escorted him downstairs. I thanked the driver for radioing for help and stepped off the bus.

The streets of the city centre were crowded with people buzzing around on their way to bars and clubs. As I turned into Hurst Street a group of white men walked past.

'Eh lads! There's that Naomi Campbell, innit? Ain't she s'posed to be wild in bed?' one of them shouted. 'Fancy a shag, love? Never had a black tart before!'

The others burst into hysterics and staggered on. I quickened my steps, anxious to get home. I was cold, exhausted and extremely fed up. I trudged past the casino, the clubs pumping out chart music and the students messing about. When I finally reached my front door, a Jamaican man, dripping with gold from head to toe, called to me from over the road.

'Yow, sexy gal! Mi waan talk to yuh.' He flashed his gold teeth but before he could say another word I ran into my flat, a fugitive under attack.

'I'm surrounded by lunatics!' I yelled at the walls, slamming the door behind me.

I lay down on my sofa and gazed up at the ceiling. The words of the drunken racist clung to me and echoed in my ears. But it was no longer *his* voice that I heard. It was the cruel, malicious voices of my schoolmates, chanting together in chorus that they didn't want a nigger in their class. I was eight years old, one of only three black children in my private school, Highfield. I'd realized I was different as soon as I arrived. The other children laughed and pointed at me, touching me as if I was a rare animal in a zoo. They'd crowd around me, pulling my long black plaits, fingering them with their dirty hands.

'Can you actually wash your hair?' they said.

I remembered one particular geography lesson. We were being taught about where different people came from. I was the only black person in the class, so they used me as an example. The teacher poked me in the chest with the sharp tip of her ruler and called me to the front. She asked the class to point out the features on me that were different to theirs and asked them if they recognized which part of the world I came from. I stood there feeling like circus entertainment as the hands of my classmates shot up one by one.

'Yes, Michael,' said Mrs Ferrill, pointing to a skinny boy.

'Well, miss,' said Michael, 'she's got a flat nose and big thick lips. Her hair is coarse like wire, so I think she's from Africa.'

'Very good, Michael, well done. Her skin is also coloured, signifying the area she comes from in the world.' My teacher pointed with her long ruler, first to a map of Africa and then at me. 'She is a Negroid. Thank you, Ebony, you may sit down now.' She ignored the sniggers of the other children.

I'd wander through the school grounds, always alone. The other children would often taunt me. 'Ape-face, what's it like to be a Negroid?' 'Were you in the Handsworth riots?' 'My mum thinks you should go back to where you come from.'

*

I sat on the floor of my clean, beautiful flat, staring at its tangerine walls, remembering the end of each school day. I would run to my mother's car, ashamed of who and what I was. Once home, I'd stare at my face in the mirror and cry, feeling cursed by my difference. I now know that I'd internalized values that crucified my self-image. But back then, at Sunday school I got down on my knees and prayed to God to be like them, to fit in, to be included and accepted. I often stood under the shower, wishing that the water would wash away all of my imperfections. I hated my 'rubber lips' and my 'Brillo pad' hair. I desperately wanted silky straight hair that shook in the wind like the other girls. I loathed my 'thunder thighs' and longed to have thin legs, like them.

My mother refused to let me feel sorry for myself. She told me that I was lucky and privileged to be in my position. 'Just keep your head held high and achieve,' she said as I sobbed. For years I hated her for not seeming to care or fight for me and for sending me to that hellish school. But as I grew older I realized she'd been fighting for me all the time and had made many sacrifices to give me the best education. My mother said racism must be fought with education, for knowledge is power. She had two jobs – nursing during the day and cleaning at night – working seven days a week until her hands were covered in blisters to give me the life, the power, the access and the opportunities that she and thousands of other black people never had. As time passed, I'd wanted to learn more about myself, who I was and where I was from, for I had been invisible in the curriculum taught to me at school.

I went into my living room and picked up books on black history and literature from my shelf, remembering how they'd helped me before. Through these books I had re-educated myself and become aware that masses of black children had experienced the same rejections as me. To my surprise, I'd discovered that there had been black kings and queens and that one of the greatest musicians, Beethoven, was a black man. I'd learned that it was black people who'd invented traffic lights, toilets and even built the mystical pyramids of Egypt. I cried when I read how my ancestors were branded and butchered as slaves, sold like cattle and robbed of their freedom, their children and their lives. I thanked them over and over again for their sacrifices as I reached new understanding and love for my people and myself.

The noise of the neighbours arguing jolted me back to the present. It was past midnight so I went to bed. Unable to sleep, I lay there and listened to the howling wind, haunted by past insults. I told myself off for being so sensitive; I needed inner peace. Something had to change. All my life I had altered my appearance to suit other people's percep-tions of 'beautiful' and by doing so I was ascribing to West-ern notions of beauty instead of my own. 'How long will you allow others to dictate and define your womanhood?' I asked myself aloud.

I got out of bed, found a pair of scissors and began cut-ting my expensive European hair extensions. I didn't stop until I had removed every strand from my head. Feeling liberated, I slept well.

Next morning. In the cold light of day, I felt naked and nervous without the hairstyle that I'd kept since leaving school, but I knew there was no going back. I combed sweet-smelling African Pride oil through my hair, defining and shaping the mass of natural curls. Instead of applying lip liner around the inside of my lips so that they appeared thinner, I smoothed my mouth with lipgloss, making it shine. I decided not to hide my legs by wearing one of my many long skirts and instead chose a pair of orange trousers that hung in the wardrobe. I'd never felt brave enough to wear them before because I was so conscious of my body, but I was surprised at how well they complemented my shapely thighs. I smiled at myself in the mirror, liking the attractive woman beaming back.

'You go, girl!' I joked, grabbing my coat.

Stepping out into a new day, I made myself a promise, speaking it like a prayer: 'I am the Invisible Woman. My needs and opinions are not heard or counted. Yet I will celebrate my unique difference and vision in a world that continues to silence, devalue and erase my history and my self.'

Rasta Love

Norman Samuda-Smith

Errol see her every week, rocking in her regular place, near to de light opposite Ital Nyah control tower. As usual, she stand up wid her two older sista dem, laughing, dancing and joking, her sista dem smoking. In Errol's eyes, she outclass dem in every way. She was a natural beauty. Nuff man love her off. Like most girls, she was going through a transition – from being a regular churchgoer, to accepting de roots and culture. Her name was Lorraine.

Errol step closer to de control tower, tek de microphone off his friend Pedro and start chat. 'Yes crowd a people, as dat musical disc steps away, is lovers rock time! I tell yuh say, come in selecta Beres!'

De lovers rock start to play and all de bredrin dem find a girl to dance wid. It seem like nobody ah talk, jus de music inna de air. Errol continued, 'As we stop to start again, tell her not to go away, cah here come de instrumental side wid my *original* lyrics as I would say . . .

'You're my days, you're my nights
I hope your kisses will make me feel so bright

131

I can see your natural beauty girl
My heart skip a beat
You turn my world
Pour your love over my heart
Make me live a likkle longer
Pour your love over my heart
You make me feel stronger . . .'

'WHOY!' was de deafening cry dat come from de dance-hall crowd, as de bredrin dem leggo dem dance partner. Errol could see Lorraine and de crowd now, punching de air wid delight, drowning his voice wid dem chanting.

'GO INNA IT ERROL!'

'GWAAN SOOPA!'

'AH WHO SEH?' Errol ask.

'GO DEH!' reply de crowd.

'Operator, I beg yuh jus get dere and stay dere!' Errol seh, as him watch Pedro mix and blend dem back inna easy skanking and more of him honey-sweet lyrics.

'AH LOVE ME AH DEAL WID!' Errol wail over de microphone as de forty-five come to an end.

Likkle did Lorraine know how special she did grow in Errol eyes. Pedro bus' out laughing. 'Is where dem lyrics come from yout' man? If yuh like de girl, grab her fe a dance and lyrics her while yuh dancing, man! She nuh know seh yuh like her.'

Errol pass de microphone back to Pedro, keeping his eyes on Lorraine de whole time. Him start mek him way through de crowd of lovers wrapped around each other, locked tight together on de dance floor. Lorraine smile at him, her pretty eyes beckoning.

Fe a yout' of seventeen, Errol was regarded as de best yout' toaster inna Birmingham, de baby of de Ital Nyah sound. When him was fourteen, him used to loaf around outside all ah de dance dat Ital Nyah did play. As Pedro,

Beres and Robbo carry in de big speaker box, Errol would offer to carry de small tweeter box dem. It come a habit dat dem never refuse him help, so soon him start get inna Ital Nyah dance free. Den dem start call Errol dem likkle box bwoy, till him learn to master de art of microphone chanting. At school, him mek sure him educate himself well – him mommy and daddy see to dat. Him leave school wid four O-Level and den him start search fe a job.

As him popularity grow even more, Errol get de opportunity fe mek guest appearance wid some ah de big man sound, like Studio City at de Chequers Night Club inna Small Heath pon a Wednesday night. Quaker City at de Rainbow Suite deh ah de city centre every Thursday, and Duke Alloy at de Tyburn House pub over inna Erdington every Sunday. Him was like a magnet, wid de talent fe turning an ailing dance into a success.

Dese big man sound try fe coax him away from Ital Nyah fe join dem, offering him de opportunity to travel nationwide to London, Manchester and Leeds; and to appear at nuff bank holiday dance in and outta town and ting. But Errol remain loyal to him bredrins Pedro, Robbo and Beres, who nurture him rise to success.

Wid dis popularity come de admirers of de feminine gender. Ital Nyah, mainly coz of Errol, have a strong female following. Him soon change him name to Pa-Pa Errol to fit de romantic side of him lyrics. Pedro, de oldest sound member, warn him bout de possible jealous man who fah woman might fancy him coz him ah mic chanter. Dese was de times when a man fear de knife as oppose to de gun. More time still, Errol being shy, despite all dat front him never mek him head swell.

Dat Friday night, when Errol leave de dance, dere was a full moon shining a silver light dat bright up de clear night sky and Jah stars. Him feel nice, like how him did get a dance wid Lorraine. De dance did sweet him. It was winter,

1974, minus six degrees and still dropping rapid, while de heavy frost dat sekkle pon de pavement was glistening. De dustman dem deh pon strike fe well over a week now. Nobody believe how much rubbish can accumulate in nine days. Every street yuh walk down, all yuh see is jus pile ah rubbish everywhere. De minèr dem a seh dem want to guh pon strike too, dat gwine lead to power cuts again; and we all know wha dat mean – no dance!

Nuff bredrin and sistren file out the dance hall on St Oswald's Road. De bredrin dem sporting dem ites, gold and green crowns, scarves and belts as dem bop wid pride along de icy pavement inna dem Clarks boots and ting. De sistren dem majestically wearing dem head-wraps in various shape, size and colour, wid dem long skirt, full-length sheepskin coat and fe dem Clarks boots, glide 'longside de bredrin dem. Every Friday night nuff ah dem would get off de number 8 bus at de Golden Hillock Road, Coventry Road junction inna Small Heath around eight. Dem destination: St Oswald's Road dance hall to hear de musical bible of Rastafari featuring Small Heath's baddess yout' sound, Ital Nyah. Dere was pure vibes every week.

De following Friday, St Oswald's was ram. Members of other yout' sounds gather to learn how fe entertain de people wid pure dub-wise and pre-release roots music. While dem listen and learn, de treble section ring inna dem ears, de bass shake dem trouziz and rattle dem ches'; de lyrics educate and mek dem meditate. Pure peace and love inna de dance as de con-gregation rock cool and easy to every rhythm dat touch down. De Ital Nyah followers stand up surrounding dem amp-case as Pedro, de operator at de control tower, mix and blend de music, teasing de crowd wid pure treble. Halfway through a tune, him give dem a full dose ah bass and it shake everyting in its path. De selector dem, Beres and Robbo, dig deep inna de record box to find a nex' hypnotizing tune, and Errol, cool and easy, chat him owna lyrics inna style and fashion dat taste like milk and honey to de dance-hall crowd.

'Yes crowd ah people, yuh tune into de baddess yout' sound, Ital Nyah sound and we nuh wear no frown! Don't f'get, tomorrow night all roads lead to St Agatha's church hall, right down dere inna Sparkbrook way! In tune to de mighty Jah Shaka from London town versus Mafia Tone Hi-Fi from Lozells! Is one fifty pon de door, security tight. So mek it a date and don't be late cah Shaka gwine trow down dub plate dat *no* other sound can imitate, seen? So nuh worry bout de energy crisis, nuh worry bout unemployment and redundancy. Don't yuh know, Jah will work it out seen? JAH!'

'RASTAFARI!' de crowd reply.

'Selassie I, ever sure, ever pure. Right about now, hol' on to de one yuh love de bes' wid out any contes'. Dis yah tune is one cut pon forty-five, stric'ly dub-wise, Gregory Isaacs, *Your Smilin Face*, trow it down, Robbo!'

De intensity calm down fe a likkle while as de bredrin dem search fe a sistren to hold a dance in de dim light.

'OOPS, excuse me selecta Robbo! Tek it slow as de love grow inna de dance hall yuh know! As we stop to start again, yuh got to grab a skirt and see what it's wort'. Got to get inna de mood, but don't be rude, jus get down and scrub . . . rub-a-dub!'

A couple of weeks go by, Errol try fe get to grips wid Lorraine. Since de night weh him did hol' her fe a dance, nutt'n nah gwaan. She was always talking to a bredda or two, cah she did know quite a few bredrins and she never find it hard fe chat wid any a dem. As a result, him get beat to de post when one bredrin decide seh him want to go out wid her. Errol look pon de rocking crowd and decide seh him nuh done wid Lorraine yet.

*

De following Monday, at Small Heath Community Centre yout' club, Errol was playing table tennis wid Pedro, and him hear de same bredrin ah talk bout Lorraine. Him never know de bredrin, true seh him was from one nedda area, but him know seh de bwoy have a bad reputation.

'At de end of de night yuh know roots, de gyal gwaan like seh she nuh want to give I nutt'n!' Errol carry on listen. De bwoy seh it arrogantly, as if it was due to him.

'So what happen den?' ask one of de roots.

'Cho, she chicken out wid some cheap double talk, man!' de bredrin seh, bathing in certainty. Errol trow down de table-tennis bat in anger.

'Nah man, yuh nuh fe talk bout de girl like dat, man!' Errol felt like him face was gwine bruk inna one million likkle piece. Him never feel so vex. De bredrin turn round.

'Den who is you, I-yah?' de bredrin ask.

Errol puff out him chest. 'Jus a man. S'pose s'maddy talk bout yuh sista like dat?'

Pedro start edge round de table, coz it look like argument ah go get weh from dem.

De bredrin step forward. 'Cho, dat different.'

'Why?'

'Yuh mus wah me cut yuh!' De bredrin reach into him pocket like seh him did have one knife in deh or someting.

Errol cuss after him. 'Yuh ignorant, man.'

'Is who yuh ah call ignorant I-yah? Me soon tump yuh inna yuh face!'

'Come nuh!'

Pedro step between dem, as Errol and de bredrin go fe each other, a crowd gather round.

'No Errol, come we go man. Come.'

'Oh, is you,' de bredrin seh. 'Jus coz yuh can chat pon de mic good, yuh feel seh yuh invincible nuh? Go-weh! Yuh ah *bwoy*!'

'Come we go rasta!' Pedro seh, guiding Errol out ah de club.

'Yeah, run weh bwoy!' de bredrin shout, laughing wid him bredrin dem.

'Don' seh nutt'n, Errol! Jus walk, dread,' Pedro seh.

'Nah man!' Errol huffing and puffing. 'Him outta order!'

'Yeah, me know him well outta order, but all dis would ah never happen if yuh did mek a move faster, dreadlocks.'

De truth was, Errol found out later dat Lorraine had successfully simmer down dat bredrin's lusting over her. She did know, deep down, him was meaning to tek advantage of her friendly nature; fe dat reason, she was branded a cock teaser.

'Mi nuh care what dem call me, me know ah nuh me dat!' she tell her two sista, who both inform her, individually, about de rumour dat a spread. 'Nutt'n never guh suh!' She was well vex. Is funny how half a story can be conceived, den believed.

Lorraine steer clear of man after dat incident. She lock herself away fe do her homework, her domestic duties, to watch TV at leisure, only setting herself free fe her school netball team. Meanwhile, her sista dem come from St Oswald's dance hall every Friday night.

'Lorraine, Oswald's was bad, man!'

'Oh really?'

'Yeah man, I mus have been ask fe a dance about fifteen time, and Errol was askin bout yuh.'

'What for?'

'Coz he like yuh.'

'Yeah, and I bet he was one ah dem dat seh I was a cock teaser, now him want to get a use.'

'Don't be stupid! In fact, Pedro tell me seh dat Errol was gwine fight fe yuh when him hear all dem man ah talk bout yuh.'

'Really?'

'Really.'

'But why? I hardly know him.'

'Well, dat nah stop him from like yuh. So wha yuh ah seh? Yuh gwine start come out again?'

'I dunno, maybe.'

Lorraine continue to stay in fe two months, till she get bored and de temptation of raving entice her back to de dance hall. Errol see her again, same finesse, rocking continually, not allowing de rumours of de past to restrict her realism. When him tek a break from de microphone dem dance nice and slow and dem talk.

'Thanks for stickin up for me.'

'No problem, I like yuh.'

'I never know yuh did. Why yuh never seh someting?'

'Coz yuh was always busy talkin, never tink yuh would be interested in me anyway.'

'I was jus bein friendly. I s'pose I learn me lesson. Man dem only jus want one ting.'

'I don't want one ting.'

'I didn't mean you.'

'Maybe yuh did, maybe yuh didn't. Where we go from here?'

'Jus gimme a while to think, Errol please. I'm still tryin to figure tings out.'

'Dat cool, I'll be waitin, seen?'

'Seen.'

As dem dance, a strange vibe was in de air, everybody look nervous and uneasy. Lorraine sense it and decide seh she want to leave de dance early. Also, de bredda dat scandalize her name was around and about. She feel seh him might follow her home and give her hassle. Errol walk her home. When him come back to de dance, him see one ambulance pull up, police was dere in force too. Pure chaos ah gwaan, sistrens running out ah de place screaming, bredrins shouting, pushing and shoving to come out. Errol force him way in against de on-comin crowd fe see wha a gwaan.

'Wha appen, Pedro?'

'Bwoy, de same bredda yuh was gwine fight de other day jus cut up a yout'. Him was lookin fe you, I-yah. I feel seh yuh bes' lay low fe a while, seen?'

'Seen.'

On de Monday at de yout' club, de same bredda cut up a nex' yout' badly, over one domino game. Some seh dem was playin fe money, and de yout' dat get cut did ah cheat, others seh him just cut de yout' fe no reason. Whatever de reason, de police couldn't mek no sense outta de attack, so dem advise de organizers of de dance and de yout' club to close down fe a cool-off period. De yout' dat get cut, jus about survive, and de bredda was sent to Borstal fe t'ree years. Entertainment inna Small Heath done!

Ital Nyah try fe mek an impact in de popular dance hall around town. Dem play de same rhythm, wid Errol chanting him original honey-sweet lyrics, but due to de lack of speaker box and ting, dem never have de wattage to produce de same quality sound in bigger places. So widout de positive vibe of de St Oswald's dance-hall scene, which was de soul food of their inspiration, dem decide dat dem gwine stop play out and rebuild and come again better than before.

Errol finally get him first job, de wage wasn't all dat good, so him decide to juggle as well by selling de works of art him draw and paint. On a Saturday afternoon inna de city centre, him choose a spot where him lay down him works. Those wid a eye fe cultural art would stop, view and buy one or two of him works of art. Him was cleaning up. One Saturday, business finish early, so Errol decide fe go home.

As he count him money and start pack him tings away, he feel one tap pon him shoulder. Him turn round.

'Lorraine! Wha appen, yuh cool?'

'Yeah, I'm fine, long time no see.'

'I know.'

Dem stare at each other fe a long time. Errol feel kinda cool and nervous de same time.

'So . . . erm . . . this is what yuh up to?' Lorraine break de silence and start browse through some of him works.

'Yeah, tryin a ting, and I have a job yuh know.'

'Have you, doin wha?'

'Workin in one warehouse storekeepin.'

'You're one ah de lucky ones.'

'Me know. De wages nuh all dat good, dat's why me ah do dis.'

'This is nice.' She hold up and view one ah him drawings.

'Yuh can have it.'

'Really?'

'Yeah man.'

'Thanks Errol.'

'No problem, so what yuh up to?'

'Nutt'n, jus doin my A-Levels at college, hard work man. Jah know.'

'So yuh jus come ah town fe do some shoppin and ting?'

'Nah man, I been tryin to get some tickets fe dis Jessus, Moambassa and Studio City dance t'night.'

Errol smile in anticipation.

'So did yuh get one?'

'No, everybody sell out.'

'I got some tickets.'

'Fe dat dance?'

'Ee-hee. Me ah chat pon de mic fe Studio City t'night.'

'Really? How many tickets yuh have?'

'Five.'

'Oh Errol, can I have t'ree please? I've never been to a big dance like dis before.'

'Serious?'

'I'm well serious, please Errol please!'

'Well dat depend on two tings.'

'What?'

'First yuh help me carry me works home.'

'Yeah OK, and de other one . . .'

'Dat yuh go out wid me t'night. Yuh ready fe dat?'

Lorraine smile. 'Seen, I'm ready.'

Lorraine sit next to Studio City control tower most of de night watching and listening to Errol hold his own against de Jessus and Moambassa toasters from London. Dem was bad mouthing him all night. Digbeth Civic Hall was ram jam. Lorraine soon find out dat dis dance was not designed for how many dance you can get, but which is de best sound playing dem baddess dub plates. It was evident dat no sound was making clear headway till Errol pick up de microphone on de seventh hour.

'When I say black people, nuff respect to selecta Blacka, de greatest selecta inna de world, Jah know! So de man play, so de king sound say. Well black people, I don't mean to brag and I don't mean to boast, coz is yuh me love de most from pillar to post yuh know. Now here come one hit bound sound to really trow yuh down, de man call Junior Delgado "Danger in Your Eyes" . . .'

De music start to play, de crowd rock. Lorraine feel hot all over, but she rock 'longside de crowd same way, and it feel good watching Errol.

'WHOY!'

'GU DEH!'

Errol bide him time.

'AH WHO SEH?!' him finally ask.

141

'GU DEH!'

'Well I play it from de top to de very las' drop. Sound call Studio City, greatest sound inna de world man. Studio City don't run competition yuh know, we nuh look nex' sound who ah look name offa we . . .'

Him start mock de odder sound, de crowd nearly dead wid laughter.

'Dem ah labba labba labba
But dem cyaan test Studio City
Dem ah run up dem mout', but dem cyaan test
    Pa-Pa Errol yuh know why?
Coz when it come to lyrics me Pa-Pa Errol well great
Me mek forty-five sound like dub plate
Me mek crowd of people tear down dance gate
Labba labba labba, but dem cyaan test Studio City . . .'

As de crowd jump up and down wid excitement, in appreciation of Errol's lyrics, Lorraine beam a proud smile and turn and seh to her sista dem.

'Dat's *my* man.'

After six months of work, redundancy catch up wid Errol. All de money him save him spend it off. Him stop selling him artwork. Him father start cuss when him locks start to grow. Him mother try her best to keep de peace between father and son.

'What time yuh come in las' night bwoy?'

'About two a clock.'

'Yuh too lie, yuh come in later dan dat.'

'Well if yuh know what time me come in, why yuh askin?'

'Coz yuh mekkin it too much of a habit.'

'I'm seventeen, Dad, me not no pickney no more!'

'While yuh livin in my house, yuh obey de rules. Yuh hear me?'

"So what's de rules den, Dad? Stay home? Don't go out? Siddung and watch telly?'

'Errol, don't talk to yuh fada like dat!' seh him mom.

'All me sayin Errol is dat ever since yuh lose yuh job, yuh party all night and now yuh ah tu'n natty dread!'

'Res' it, Dad.'

'No, me nah res' it. How yuh expect fe get a job when yuh head stay suh?'

'There's no jobs out deh, Dad. Yuh read de paper every day and yuh watch de news. Englan mash up, dem soon put yuh pon t'ree day a week.'

'Dat is my problem, you nah try.'

Errol start to laugh one sarcastic laugh. 'Even before me start locks up, I been tryin. Nobody nuh wah gimme no job.'

'Cho, ah foolishness dat yuh ah talk.'

'Yuh want me to spell it out fe yuh, Dad? Aright. I go fe one job right, I put on me suit and tie, jus like how school, you and Mom teach me. I look smart, I act smart. Den me see one white bwoy turn up inna one T-shirt and dutty jeans, wid one tattoo all de way up him arm. Him get de job not me. *Why?*'

'You tell me why.'

'Coz in dis climate dem call de recession, they lookin after dem owna people. Black people jus haffi step aside and draw dole money. Dem nuh want to call me English and me born yah!'

Errol father shake him head in disagreement, him mother look 'fraid.

'No Errol,' him father seh. 'Yuh nuh fe look at tings dat way son.'

'Is not me, is dem. Dad, let me tell yuh. England's streets nuh pave wid gold wid plenty work deh bout no more. Dat done. Yuh see me now, my locks gwine grow long inna Babylon, and me gwine play me sound system and get pay. Me nah guh siddung and wait fe nobody fe gimme a job or money.' Errol well vex. Him never like talk to him father so, but de situation bu'n him.

'Errol, calm down nuh!' him mom seh.

'Cho, me gone. Oonoo nah listen.'

'Where yuh goin now?'

'OUT!'

'ERROL, COME BACK HERE!'

'Leave him, Malcolm.'

Errol slam de front door and head off to de community centre. Him feel seh dat a few game of table tennis or five-a-side football will get rid of de aggression dat was flowing through him veins. De yout' club had reach de end of its ban and open again soon after him lose him job. Errol never see Lorraine fe de last six weeks due to her exams and ting. On dis particular Wednesday, her college netball team have a game against de local community centre team. Errol was loafing about in de yout' club when him hear de lyrics from a couple ah bredrin.

'Yow, dis fit netball team ah play outside yuh know.'

'Yuh lie!'

'Nah man, a serious ting, Jah know!'

So all de bredrins run downstairs to view de dawtas on court in dem short netball skirt, and to shout a few rude remarks whenever a dawta flash a firm leg. Errol was silent, him eyes was on Lorraine. Him intention, reason wid her when de game done.

She was surprise wid him change in appearance, but she tink seh de dreads suit him, dem mek him look cultured and compelling.

'Did yuh enjoy de game?'

Errol shrug him shoulders. 'Mmm, it was aright.'

'What's wrong?'

'Why is it when we find an identity fe ourselves, everybody want to chant it down?'

'Yuh have an argument wid yuh dad?'

'Yeah. How you know?'

'Me too. Him don't like de dance I'm going to. Him seh, him never come ah dis country fe see me tu'n rasta.'

'Same ting me dad jus tell me. What you seh to dat?'

'I never seh nutt'n to him. But I believe dat if it wasn't for Rastafari and roots music, we wouldn't be reading de Bible now. We wouldn't believe in nutt'n.'

'And we wouldn't know bout Marcus Garvey . . .'

'And William Gordon . . .'

'And Paul Bogle . . .'

Lorraine gave Errol a hug.

'I want you to know dis, no matter what happen between us, everyting's gonna be aright.'

De dates come thick and fast. Errol put on him best Cecil Gee tops and tailor-made trouziz. Him tek Lorraine fe see Gregory Isaacs, Dennis Brown and Fred Locks. Dem go to de midnight dance and de Shaka dance, Coxsone, Mafia Tone and Duke Alloy. Nuff entertainment, nuff excitement. But as dem love start fe tek full bloom, Lorraine mother and father find out dat Errol is a dread.

'Lorraine, Mrs Morgan down de road tell me seh you and one natty head bwoy ah stan pon street corner more dan once. Is true?' seh her mother.

'Yeah, is true.'

'Jesus Chris' have mercy!'

'So what's wrong wid dat?' Lorraine ask.

'All dem do is smoke ganja, rob, steal and lay about.'

'Not my man.'

'Man? What yuh know about man? Dem deh bwoy no

145

good yuh know. Dem have no ambition,' seh her father.

'He's got plenty ambition believe me.'

'Plenty ambition nuh? Before you know it, yuh gwine come in yah wid a belly. Den what yuh gwine do when him nuh want yuh?'

'He's not like dat, Mom.'

'Girl, nuh bodda gimme no back chat!'

Dem stop her from goin out completely. Wid de help of her sista dem, Errol and Lorraine mek a plan to meet at de corner of her street one Friday night. Errol stan' up waiting fe her to come.

'Mom, I done me homework, I'm jus goin over to de club, all right?'

'Gyal, find yuh self back in yah! Me know seh yu ah try sneak out fe go meet dat deh natty head bwoy! Yu nah go no weh!'

Errol check de time pon him watch, 9.30 p.m. It was bitter cold. Him bounce around trying to keep warm, while doing dat, him compose a lyric out loud.

'De night is dark, de weather is cold
I feel seh she can't come
So me ah stand yah alone
Ah kick rockstone
I feel seh she can't come
How she leave me inna de street?
Dress all slick and neat
When de music out dere is fine
Wid de treble and bass line
I feel seh she can't come . . . CHO!'

Lorraine never turn up. Errol start mek him way home. Him cold. Him vex. Him heart bruk.

'ERROL, WAIT!'

Him turn around and see Lorraine sista dem running toward him.

'Where's Lorraine?'

'Mom and Dad won't let her out. She seh everyting's gonna be aright.'

'So dem ah fight 'gainst de natty.'

'Seen.'

'Where you two goin now?'

'Oswald's, man.'

'Oswald's open back up? Who ah play?'

'You and Ital Nyah, rasta.'

Errol enter de dance hall to see and hear a rebuilt Ital Nyah, entertaining dem biggess crowd fe months. Pedro smile as him hand de mic to a sad Pa-Pa Errol.

Errol look pon Lorraine sista dem, wishing dat she was dere, laughing, dancing and joking. Den him realize seh him might not see her again.

Him start chant.

'Yes crowd of people! Ital Nyah and Pa-Pa Errol is back! We gwine play yuh musical tracks from our record racks. Hear my lyrics when I tell yuh. Inna me, lyrics inna me. Lyrics inna me coz ah well vex yuh see! Her momma lock de door, her poopa keep de key, dat's what stop her from lovin me.'

'WHOY!'

'GU INNA IT ERROL!'

'BOW BOW BOW BOW!'

Errol tek a deep breath and decide seh him nah go bawl. Him look pon de crowd and see how dem ah smile after him, like dem love him off. Him smile back.

'Yeah man, I remember sweet Lorraine.'

Chrysalis

Ifemu Omari

Over the centuries, many mothers have killed their children to save them from life. This is nature's edict. It is quite common in the animal kingdom. The black widow spider gorges her own eggs; the common seal often devours her newborn pups. Even the domestic cat may eat her own kittens. Why? Because of a mother's fear.

My son died today.

'It's a boy!' they chorused. 'Yula, you have a son!'

I heard their voices from far away. I was too tired to say anything. I watched them watching me. Changing expressions, secret codes, different songs. They whispered to each other.

They gave me my wrapped baby. On his wristband: *James*. They said I'd been quiet too long, that the baby needed feeding and a name. So they wrote James on his wristband.

'You can change it if you like,' whispered the white nurse. 'Who wants to name such a lovely bundle after some fuddy-duddy dead king?' She smiled. Dirty chipped teeth. 'So whaddaya say, sweetie?'

I was too exhausted to answer. She took my baby from me and gave it to someone else who I couldn't see through the white-blue light. I gasped as I watched a needle spit a sharp fountain of fluid. She leaned towards me. Dirty chipped teeth, stale breath. Sweat mixed with perfume. I swooned. Stillness.

I sit in our quiet house. I close my eyes and cup my hands over my face, searching for a retreat. Questions are clamouring noisily in my head. What do I do now? Telephone his friends, his fiancée, the surgery? Make a list? Stay calm. Why is this happening? My father used to say, 'There is order and God's reason in everything.' Dear God, this is the wrong way round.

There's a bang. I look up to see the mouth of the letterbox spewing today's ration of envelopes into a brown and white pile. How long have I been sitting here? The glare of the morning sun pouring through the kitchen window hurts my eyes.

This is still the same morning.

'Your son didn't suffer, Mrs Miller. It was a head-on collision.' The hospital consultant, a lanky, blond-haired man. He'd stooped towards me to murmur the bad news. I stared at him. He was about James's age.

'Your mother must be a very proud woman,' I whispered.

'Mrs Miller, I'm very sorry . . . I understand from my colleagues that your son, Doctor Miller, practised locally. This must be an awful shock for you. Is there anything I can do for you? A cup of tea? Contact a relative?'

'A taxi . . . please get me a taxi.'

He seemed relieved, pleased at my response as if I'd released him from some awful trap. He hurried away, his white coat flapping like a seagull's wings preparing for flight.

*

This is still the same morning. I look at the kitchen clock with its large white face and bold numerals. Five, ten, fifteen . . . sixty-five minutes. I have been a mother without a child for one hour and five minutes. A childless mother. God's cruel joke.

Our kitchen has creamy yellow cupboards and sky grey walls. He liked grey; I liked yellow. So we said we'd have both. Laughter burst out in our home like a party of swallow-tailed butterflies, raining down their crimsons, indigos, ochres, settling on us like a single, colourful robe.

What should I do now? There must be something I can do. The hallway is full of unopened envelopes and I've been sitting in my coat all this time. I try to unbutton the collar but my hands are heavy and feel as if they don't belong to me. I begin to walk towards the front door, but it's as if the door is moving towards me. The smooth fabric of my coat caresses my knees. I spread the envelopes on the kitchen table like a pack of magician's cards.

What kind of God would take a good man's life? 'The wicked will feel God's wrath on this earth.' That was another of my father's sayings. When he didn't get his own way. My father acting like God. A pompous, self-righteous God. Taking my son as punishment.

'I hate you and your God!' I scratch at the air. 'You and your damned God! *Give me back my son!* Give him back to me, give him back to me!'

If only it could be yesterday. I would find a way for me and James, like I did before. If only I could sleep back into yesterday.

It was a strangely cold July night. I waited and waited on the draughty platform. The trains were leaving platform eight, Birmingham New Street, for Manchester Piccadilly every hour on the half-hour. Three trains had gone and Adrian still hadn't arrived. He only had to travel from Handsworth Wood. Perhaps he'd gone to the wrong platform. I skipped up the stony stairs three by three, backwards and forwards between platforms. Four hours later I was tired. I was an expert witness to people's private moments, goodbyes and hellos all the same. A scraggy, one-eyed dog lay next to his master's leg by the men's toilet. He spied me wearily, yawned and closed his one eye. Maybe Adrian never got my letters. A new thought, as the tannoy announced in a stiff Birmingham accent: 'The ten thirty to Manchester Piccadilly is now approaching platform eight.' I turned and caught a glimpse of a friend of my father's. He was marching towards the exit, clad in British Rail blue. I tucked my head into my coat and held on to my upturned collar, ran down the steps towards the shrill of whistles. I almost knocked a guard over, prising at the train door.

'I'm sorry,' I said. 'I just can't miss this one.'

'Be more careful next time, miss,' he said mildly. He shut the door again, blew on his whistle.

The train was one of those old trains that I'd seen in black and white movies: where lovers elope and goodies in white trilbies and baddies in black ones chase one another. I chose an empty compartment and pulled the sliding door open. The effort made me feel faint. I sat down. The high-backed, musty brown check seats were fitted with mahogany panels and had no doubt seen grander days. It was a No Smoking cabin but its mustiness was mixed with the smell of nicotine. I looked out into the darkness of the window at my sad reflection. I'd combed my hair into an Afro to make me look older. Corn-rowing or any kind of plaits took the hair back off my face and exposed a young schoolgirl. My face was thinner than I remembered it. Skin paler, eyes almost bulging.

151

The train hissed into the night. *Shhh . . . don't tell anyone
. . . don't tell anyone.*

I knew very little about my lover. His name was Adrian. He
was a sixth-former and known to be very clever. He didn't
keep company with anyone. Maybe he was an only child.
He had no brothers or sisters at the school. I'd watched him
from a distance; satchel thrown carelessly over his shoulder,
red tie loosely knotted around his open-necked white shirt.
He seemed so bold, so adult, so attractive. Our occasional
exchange of words sent my heart into giddy questioning.
What did Adrian mean when he said . . .? What was Adrian
implying when he asked . . .? That's when I began to keep a
diary, to put my secret somewhere. Reading my dreams over
and over again gave me hope. My parents probably found
the diaries with their made-up stories after I was gone. Better
that than the truth: two lustful kids groping loose in the
dark. Only a few moments of clumsy fumbling in a badly
lit corner of the playground, then it was over. Not even a
kiss. Then his voice, distant in the dark.

'Don't tell anyone, promise?'

'Promise,' I said. And he was gone.

My diary was full of promises.

*17th: Today you told me that I was the most beautiful girl in
the school and although you hardly ever speak to me now it's cos
our secret is so special and people get so jealous and we don't
want to let them spoil it for us. So my darling I will keep our
precious secret and won't tell anyone not even my best friend.
Promise.*

I had missed three periods before I understood I was
pregnant.

My parents were the kind of people everyone looked up to.
They were both from Jamaica. Mum came from an educated

family. She was light-skinned and was only allowed to marry Dad after she graduated from Morant Bay High School. Her family didn't approve of her choice. Dad was black-skinned and had left school in the sixth grade to work as a carpenter. Mum wanted to be a nurse.

In spite of the rumours of Dad's drinking and womanizing, Mum was very excited when he came to her house in his starched white shirt and razor-sharp trousers to ask my grandfather for her hand in marriage. Mum had graduated that very morning. I loved it when she told me that story.

Dad often said that I was growing too big, too fast. He said that Mum was treating me like a grown woman because she had no woman friends of her own.

'Mind what you're sowing, Clariss,' he said to her. 'The crop might be too big for you to reap on your own.' Dad often talked in proverbs. He was a Bible man who rarely went to church. The church was full of hypocrites, he said. 'Betting shop, marking pools, dominoes, any form of gambling on the weekend, shebeen on a Saturday night and church on a Sunday,' he said.

'That's going too far now, Theo,' Mum insisted.

'Going too far? You're the one with the upbringing. It's like you gone too far in the ways of these people. But I'm the one with the standards, and those are the standards that Yula and Harold will follow. My standards, woman. Not yours.'

They'd arrived in Birmingham, newly-weds, his carpenter's certificates stored neatly in a long brown envelope. But Dad eventually settled for work as a porter with British Rail. His new work mates called him Sonny. They said his name was too fussy. Dad tolerated English people. He loved the English language. His Bible, his correspondence course and the *Sunday Telegraph* were his higher education.

Mum worked at the hospital. She was still training to

153

become a nurse. She also made clothes for whoever would buy them. She cut her own patterns and was down the Bull Ring every other Saturday buying the most fashionable material. Mum could cut any style. She said the secret was in the pressing: press every seam as you go along to make the material lie flat against the body. Mum even got orders from white people. 'Mrs Miller,' they'd say, 'your dresses compete with any high street store.' Summer was her busiest period because she sewed school uniforms for me and my brother and classrooms of poor children in our area.

Mum and Dad tried their best to do right by us. My world was school, church and back yard, my younger brother Harold and a handful of church friends.

Only Harry dared to test the rigid boundaries our father set for us. Like the day he sneaked out to play marbles with some bigger boys on the street. Dad watched him go. He took his leather belt and laid it carefully on his folded *Sunday Telegraph*. Then he strode quietly into the kitchen to look over the meat Mum had left cooking while she popped out.

An hour later, as the leather licked Harry, my father chided him rhythmically.

'No disobedience –'

Thwack.

'– no shame –'

Thwack.

'– in my house!'

10th: My period used to come on tenth or eleventh each month. Is it seventh or eighth month now? Not sure! Belly is like a football.

16th: Found way of hiding belly. Been wearing cousin Esme's hand-me-downs. She's much bigger than me. Her tank tops and midi skirts so fitted on her, make me look like a coat-hanger. Good. Dad approves of me in her clothes. Says I look respectable.

23rd: How much longer can I hide belly? Can't talk to Mum.

She'll get in trouble with Dad. Dad's beaten Harry again! Just for playing out. No answer from Adrian. I've written three times now.

So I, Yula Miller, first child of two and only daughter of Theophilious Harold Miller and Clariss Lee Miller, ran away to a northern town that I spotted in an atlas of Great Britain, six inches away from the Midlands, taking my belly of shame with me.

The train halted suddenly. I got up. The walls of my womb burst, water gushing forth as I hit the floor. I saw reds, yellows, blues, like lights moving at a fairground. I wanted to vomit, to empty myself, to start again.

Goodness and mercy, all my days. Amen. Mummy, I'm so sorry.

'Too late for sorry, girl! You'll soon be sorry! Look at you, and still a schoolgirl! We didn't fight to hold our head up for little sluts like you to let us down.'

'You're not my mother!'

A black hand slapped my face.

'Thank God for that,' said the nurse. 'Now sit up and drink the tea. It's getting cold and your little bastard is only a couple of hours away. Mind you, if you're lucky it might be stillborn.'

'Audrey, don't be so cruel! The young lady's had a harrowing time! You've lost a lot of blood, sweetie.' That was the other nurse. She was white.

'Young she is, but lady she's not,' retorted Audrey, marching off.

'Don't mind her, sweetie. She's going off shift now. She's just a bit tired of seeing so many unmarried coloured girls in your condition.' The white nurse tucked the sheets around me. 'We're proud of her, really. She's the only coloured Sister we have and she's the strictest one in the entire hospital.

Sister Audrey Johnson takes her job very seriously.'

James was born three hours later, just before the white nurse, whose name was Valerie, went off shift.

The Dwights were there every time I woke up. Offering kind words, encouraging me to hold James. I couldn't help the thoughts in my head. The baby was marked; perhaps they'd marked him. Perhaps this baby wasn't even my baby. Perhaps it was the Dwights' devil child. The child they couldn't have, the child that they made me have. Mr Dwight looked at Mrs Dwight and smiled a wolf smile. Chiselled teeth, their shining hurt my eyes. Mrs Devil pursed her snake lips and said nothing.

'Take him away!' My voice screamed around me.

'Never mind, it's Valerie. I'm here now.' Glistening steel spitting the perfect fountain. 'I'm here now.' And she was. Valerie and I, a slip of a girl, dancing with butterflies.

Valerie said the Dwights were good people who'd helped unmarried mothers before. She said they really liked James and that he was the first child they'd offered to foster. As I was underage this would be a great help to me.

Fostering was simple, Valerie said: 'It'll give you a break every fortnight, sweetie, help you to cope. D'you understand?' I nodded vaguely. 'A social worker will explain it better in a few days. It's for the best, you'll see, sweetie. A fresh start,' she assured me.

It was just as Valerie said. A few days later, an oldish woman with a professional smile, a pile of papers and a silver Parker pen introduced herself at my bedside. My social worker, Mrs Sherrington. She told me exactly the same things Valerie had but in her brisk way of talking. No hums, no haas, no kindly reassurances.

'Now sign here, dear, it's the best you can do for James.'

She handed me several sheets of paper and her pen. She pointed to the last line, indicating where I should sign.

'They're duplicates, dear. These two are for Laurel Place, where you and your little boy will live. Just sign it twice.'

I did so, and gave the sheets to her outstretched hands.

'And that' – pointing to the form she'd slipped on to my lap – 'is to safeguard your son's future. Sign twice on the last page.'

The Dwights had already signed. Precise, tiny handwriting complemented the bold print of the words 'Foster Parents'. The weight of the pen made me write my name larger than usual and beside the small printed word 'mother' I wrote: 'Yula Miller, MOTHER'.

Mrs Sherrington folded the forms neatly and patted them on her lap. 'Well, that's that. Good girl. Time to go.' No goodbyes. No Valerie.

James was six weeks old when we left the hospital. Mrs Sherrington drove us to our new home. In the back of her car I held James and nervously read the bright leaflet she'd given me: 'Laurel Place, a long-stay hostel, is a unique project designed to give real stability to disadvantaged mothers.'

It sounded so poetic.

Laurel Place was an overcrowded den of stray young females trying to make sense of their plight while coping with their unplanned offspring. The girls prowled around; ignorant, angry and hateful. We were at war. Like Sophie who let me know I was a bad mum without actually saying it. I glared at her. She tried to defend herself. She was a stringy, freckle-faced redhead from London. Bitten nails. Pink nail varnish.

'Ain't me sayin it, Yules. But you gotta admit it's strange that you're the only one.'

'What else are they saying about me?'

'The usual. That you're a bit weird.'

Another stabbing look from me. She became weaker and more erratic.

'It's not me, Yules. Honest!'

When I got back to my room with my mug of hot chocolate I could still hear her cooing. I thought of my dad. These days his proverbs seemed to make sense. All the other girls had been sent to Laurel Place by their parents. I was the only self-referral.

I kept myself to myself. They left signs of themselves all over the place, like cats spraying. Hair in the bath usually meant Caroline. In the shower, either Sophie or Janet. Pink lipsticked cigarette ends in the sink was definitely Janet; red lipstick was Sophie, but red lipstick and in saucers was Caroline. And so on. I didn't smoke and the fumes made me wheeze. Why was it that only James had foster parents? Was I the only bad mother there? I supposed that if I left James and went discoing like Caroline that would make me a good mother. After all, she didn't have foster parents carting off *her* daughter every two weeks.

I never did like the Dwights, even after I came out of hospital. They were always smiling.

'Tea, Yula?'

'Yes, thank you.' I played along. *When in the lion's mouth . . .* Dad used to say.

'Where did we go yesterday, James?' said Mrs Dwight.

'Auntie Aggie, Aggie . . . me –'

'Who's *Auntie* Aggie?' I interrupted.

'My sister Agnes,' Mrs Dwight said calmly.

'Mummy, *Mummy*!' James shouted.

'Now, now, James. Don't be impolite and do sit up straight, dear,' said Mr Dwight.

James went quiet. He was only two. 'Auntie Aggie . . . circus, the circus. Broom, broom!' he said, holding on to an imaginary steering wheel with both hands. 'Mummy and Daddy not come.'

China crashed, mustard-coloured stains spat on their white tablecloth. My teacup.

'Never mind, dear.'

Said the spider to the fly, I thought.

'It will wash out.' Mrs Dwight smiled at me. The perfect hostess. She picked up the pieces.

The tea-party ritual was the same every weekend. After tea they sent James to his room and he came back dressed in the clothes I'd bought him from the charity shop. The pure cottons and drills and corduroys that identified my child as theirs were left in a neat little pile on a neat little bed with Laura Ashley wallpaper, curtains, bedspread. I could only ever experience that kind of luxury flipping through *Home and Garden* magazines in the doctor's surgery. This was their home; theirs and James's.

They drove me and James home in silence. The Dwights' gold Vauxhall Viva crawled up in front of Laurel Place like a hearse. We lived in one room. *James's charity clothes suit this area*, I thought. He didn't look like my child in all that luxury. Poverty smells ugly, like rotting fish.

'Thank you, Mr and Mrs Dwight,' I said as James climbed out of the car.

'Take good care of yourself, my dear. James, be good for Mummy, now.'

James giggled and bounced up the stairs of the once grand building, with its huge pillars of grey, peeling paint. By the time I'd wrenched the key from the front door and bundled him into the communal kitchen, his joy had dissipated.

'So you have a new mummy and daddy now, have you?' I dumped him into one of the dark brown plastic chairs. I hated the sound of my voice.

'Me no daddy!'

'But you've always had a mummy,' I said.

James was silent, head bowed. He said, 'Me sleepy.'

'You weren't sleepy fifteen minutes ago with the Dwights, were you, James? *Were* you?' His silence fired my anger. 'I'm talking to you. You've got more than enough to say to a couple of toffee-nosed strangers, but nothing to your own mother? I'm *talking* to you!'

The ceiling boomed. I must've woken Caroline. Her room was above the kitchen.

'Will you bloody well keep the noise down!'

Her little girl started to cry. I could hear her plod across the floor to get the child from the cot, then plod back to her bed, muffled sounds as she cuddled her daughter under the blankets.

Sniffling sounds. James cried, his head still low.

'Oh, go to bed, James.' I was exasperated. He dragged his feet across the fake-wood lino landing.

I went to the fridge to take out the chicken I'd defrosted for the next day. The cellophane was broken and there were pieces missing. I put what was left in a white Tupperware container. Frustration and fury mixed in with chopped onions and garlic. I could hear James crying. What to do? I knew the thief. It had to be Caroline. Confront her or comfort my son? Caroline would deny everything as usual. Her new Bay City Rollers scarf and that half-dozen LPs had probably eaten away her weekly allowance, she was stealing food. I could hear her denial already: 'I bought the LPs weeeeks ago, an' the scarf was a present from my mum.' 'Liar,' I would say, and there would be an almighty scrap. I was exhausted. Better to keep the peace. I chopped more onions with my meat knife.

James seemed to be howling. The howling was around me, moving like a tornado all the way from the room we shared, wrapping around me like a huge plastic bandage.

I began to sing a song that James liked. '"Oranges and lemons," said the bells of St Clements. "When will you pay me?" said the bells of Old Bailey.'

The smell of onions stung my eyes.

'"When I get rich," said the bells of Shoreditch.'

The Dwights are rich white people. Can't have children of their own. So they want to take mine. He seemed so happy, giggling with them. Then he stopped laughing when he came home with me. And now he won't stop howling. My tears are burning. My slippers are slip-slop-slipping against the fake wood floor. Our bedroom door is opening. Creaking. No one ever bothers to oil the doors here. Little things never seem to matter for poor people.

The howling tornado is engulfing me.

'*Mummy, mummy, no, no!*'

Dull, heavy hoofs against the lino floor.

'What the fuck are you doing?'

'Put the knife down, Yula!'

'Yula, give Caroline the knife!'

'Janet, phone the police, now! Sophie, stay! Don't leave!'

'"When will you pay me?" say the bells of Old Bailey.'

'She's doolally, I told you, she's stark raving mad!'

'Caroline, shut up.' Sophie was whispering. There was fear in her voice. No fear in Caroline's voice.

'Caroline,' I whispered. 'Why did you steal my chicken? Again and again, you steal my things.'

'What? You're crazy. I haven't!'

'The truth, Caroline!' The howling had stopped, the tornado was gone. I felt calm. 'You spent your allowance on Bay City Rollers LPs and a tartan scarf. I saw them.'

'Just tell her the truth, Caroline, and give her back her chicken!'

'Shut your fucking mouth, Sophie. Whose side are you on?' Fear in Caroline's voice now.

'*Shut your fucking mouth, Sophie, whose side are you on?*' I mimicked. 'The truth, Caroline!'

'I haven't got your silly chicken, you mad cow! I bought the LPs weeks ago,' she said.

There were singing sirens and blue lights flashing on our bedroom curtains. I sat down on the edge of my son's bed.

'Where's James?' I heard my voice ask.

'Now, miss, don't be silly. I'm Officer Meadows. Please give me the knife.'

'Officer, officer! She tried to stab her son! She would've if we hadn't come in on time! She was going to stab him!' Caroline was crying.

'Where's James?' I said.

Whispers.

I gave the policeman the knife. He put his arms around me and led me back to the kitchen. 'Let's have a nice cup of tea, shall we? Your social worker will be here soon. James's foster parents will look after him for a little while.'

'Yes, thank you.'

'I'm going to press charges! She was going to kill her son, and then me, and all for two fuckin pieces of chicken!'

Caroline was still screaming.

What kind of God? A good man's life, and for what reason? 'The wicked will feel God's wrath on this earth,' Dad said when he didn't get his own way with things. When I was little I believed in the power of prayer. I prayed for him to die. Every night for a whole month, but it didn't work. I wonder how Harry is doing; whether he got married; whether he's a good man; whether he pleased our father.

They never told me they were proud of me. I got to tell James I was proud of him. Over and over until he laughed and told me to stop. He came back to me. He forgave me everything.

*

All those eyes were looking at me when the policewoman put a blanket around my shoulders and led me down the steps. All the people who'd made up the story of my life since I'd become a mother. They watched me go: Sophie, Janet and Caroline huddled at the top of the stairs. Caroline's eyes were smiling. I darted her a look and she burst into tears. The Dwights stood by their car with their matching, endearing snake-smiles, holding James tight, as if they had been given ownership of a stray dog. They stroked his hair.

'Get better, Mummy. Mummy, get better . . .'

'Don't upset yourself, James.' They both stroked his head.

The letter that came to 9 Rosewood Cottage would change my life again. There were no roses and no wood, but I'd been moved between so many pretty names, and for once I was happy. I hibernated for years, waking occasionally when news of James came by letter. I was classed as a twenty-four-hour dependent. They said that I had lost my voice. Truth was, I'd willed myself silent. There was no point. No one cared to listen.

From time to time, some busybody auxiliary would read one of James's letters to me. Then they would toss it care-lessly on my bed. The letters were about his university days, his travels and his years of medical school in America. My son was doing fine. He made only scant mention of the Dwights. Mr Dwight had died five years before. He was cremated and Mrs Dwight had wanted no flowers. Only James and Mrs Dwight and the pastor were at the funeral. This last letter said Mrs Dwight had died. There was no need to explain that only James and the pastor had been present.

The real news was that James was coming to visit. My joy threatened to betray me. I wanted to laugh and skip and jump and play. Three days after the letter arrived I heard

Nancy, the manager, speaking with the high-pitched voice she reserved for strangers and important visitors.

'She can't speak. We've not found anything medically wrong. It's been years, although we can always tell if there's something she's not happy about!'

I heard the listener chuckle. It was such a distinguished chuckle.

'Mama, are you still giving trouble?' His words kissed my ears. He smelled fresh, clean and decent. I didn't look up. Was he alone?

'Mama, hold my hand. We need to talk. I know you can talk, Mama. Mama, I've got plans for us. I'm here to take care of you, Mama.'

The tears welled in the little gully of my hands, like a warm, grateful spring. His voice was different. Velvet soft, deep. Memories; torn, stitched, patched. Only a few years with my son and yet his voice made it sound so beautiful.

My son drove me away from Rosewood Cottage. The journey was very long. James never stopped talking, singing, chatting, making jokes. I slept on his voice and the rhythm of the car. He told me that he liked Mr Dwight better than Mrs Dwight. They'd tried to foster another black child, but they were told it was inappropriate. Mrs Dwight was furious and she wrote to her local MP. James chatted and chatted. I was jolted awake by the stillness of the car.

'We're here, Mama. Our home.'

Our house. It was big. Eight windows and flower baskets hanging between each window. Roses and wood. James opened the door and let me out of the car as if I was royalty. I laughed and laughed until I cried. I cried on the broad shoulders of my only child. My son.

'Yes, Mama. Cry your heart out and give thanks. You're home.'

*

I awake in the same place, the same day. My eyes are burning red as if I haven't slept for months. My sleep was deep, but time seems to be moving under its own heavy burden.

I walk towards the phone, wearisome. I dial the number I've known all my life. There's a different ringing tone on the line. Someone picks up the phone. I recognize his voice.

'Hello, Dad. It's me, Yula.'

'*Yula?*'

'My son is dead, Dad. He died today.'

Battle of Wills

Rubina Din

It was turning into a clear evening. The air was chilled. Sun red gashed across the darkening sky as a car pulled up outside a dingy little house in the middle of a terraced street, only yards away from the local infants school. A young, frail-looking woman turned off the ignition and sat still while the sun continued to fade. The woman got out of her car, tripping in her haste. She stood and looked up into the sky, which seemed to be in the middle of a bloody battle – with the sun losing.

A muffled noise broke her concentration. Saira stared back towards the car, towards the still-fastened carrycot. She opened the car door and dragged out the Asda bags surrounding the cot. The noise became louder as the pile of bags on the pavement grew. Cries echoed in the silence. Saira ignored them and walked to her front door, loaded. She dropped the bags and looked up again at the frayed sky. She found her keys amid a mass of squashed receipts and watched the door swing open. Turning back to the road, she noticed a woman; hunched up by the chill in the air, watching her. She seemed disgusted but Saira was too tired to care.

The cries from the car became agonized. Suddenly concerned, Saira lifted out the carrycot and untangled Shaan from his covers. The noise stopped. A very red-faced little boy looked up into her eyes, scrubbing his damp face. He smiled sweetly up at her, beautiful despite his sore cheeks.

Saira's eyes filled with tears.

Weighed down by the cot, she staggered into the house, through the blue front room – its plants trailing from the ceiling to the floor – into the cold living room. Dumping the carrycot on the floor, she rushed back to collect the bags. Once outside, she sighed deeply, making her feel light-headed. She heard the call to prayer ringing in the air as she ran to the car and slammed the door shut, then hooked a grocery bag on to every finger available so she wouldn't have to make a second journey. She trudged in. Shaan sat talking to himself, very contentedly. The pleasant picture made her smile.

She switched on the lights and lit the gas fire. New life flickered in her eyes as the flames warmed her; a glow spread across her face. She looked down at the dull, grease-stained carpet, grabbed Shaan clear of it and threw herself down on to the musty settee. It smelled of baby sick. They played for a few moments, both happy and alert. Shaan's eyes lit up from a dull brown to a dark velvet. Then a frown crossed her face. She put Shaan down on the settee. He wriggled to the edge. She pushed him back; he edged forward, pleased with himself and the game. She stopped, stared at him for a moment and hurried to the kitchen, leaving him precariously balanced but content.

Even though the Council had spent a lot of money on the house, the smell of rotting wood was strong. She knew it would be a few moments before her nose adjusted. A mouse scuttled across the carpet. Saira held her breath.

'Bloody mice,' she said, her heart in her mouth.

She resigned herself to the ever-present mice and mixed Shaan's milk. As she entered the living room she sniffed, wiping the rotten smell away. She panned the room; by now Shaan would be hiding under a pile of clothes – she knew her son. Just in time she saw that he hadn't made it yet – he was still teetering on the edge of the settee. She grabbed him and stuffed the bottle into his tiny mouth. His tongue pushed it out. She stuffed it in. His tongue pushed it out. The battle continued. Finally, Shaan began to suckle the bottle. Saira seemed to have won. The milk disappeared slowly.

The angry lines on Saira's face smoothed out as she sat the baby up to burp him. Shaan smiled a watery little smile. Saira smiled back. Shaan threw up all over himself, her, the settee and the carpet. Saira smacked his bottom and pushed him back on to the settee. The baby screamed, his lungs clear and loud. She cried and cursed, curses she used every day when feeding. The baby stopped howling abruptly; perhaps he was used to the routine. The mother stopped rocking her body. She lifted her face from her hands and, in a gush of sympathy, hugged the child close to her breasts, crying into his milk-stained face.

But when she lifted her face from his, the settee, the floor, the baby and his clothes were all still covered in vomit.

The front door opened.

Saira held her breath. Automatically, she turned round as the living-room door opened. Her expression changed from tenderness to stone.

It was Tariq, of course. He scanned the dishevelled room as if he was in a stranger's house. A white carrier bag containing a gallon of milk swung at his thigh. His mouth opened and closed like a fish as he retched. He fumbled in his pocket, pulling out a tissue to cover his nose.

Saira watched. His thin, unshaven face turned towards

her. He moved closer, towering over the seated figure. The baby cooed gently to himself, playing with his chubby feet.

'Is he OK?' Tariq asked.

She looked at the floor, ignoring him; the smell no longer affected her. She counted the different types of lumps in the baby sick.

Again he asked, looking at the playing child, 'Is he OK?'

Saira got up and walked towards the kitchen, her body tense. But Tariq was faster; he grabbed hold of her shoulders so she had to face him. Her head moved to indicate the hands, her face tight and harsh. His eyes followed the glance and he dropped his hands. She glared at him, the tightly wound cogs in her head unwinding at top speed.

'Does he bloody look like he's all right?' she said.

Tariq's fists tightened. He looked around, pausing at different points in the room. Shaan's yellow rattle lay on the floor near the fire – its colour seemed too vibrant. Tariq's face puffed, becoming redder. He took a deep breath, angry and puzzled. 'I'm only asking because I'm trying to be the father you want me to be.'

'You make me sick,' she spat. 'You have no bloody brain of your own. You always need others to tell you what to do.'

She placed her hand on the clammy kitchen doorknob, then wiped her fingers on her dress. She left Tariq muttering to himself, but was not surprised when he followed her. *Just leave me alone*, she thought, swinging round, a jar of sugar in her hand. She threw it at him. The jar missed by inches and smashed against the kitchen wall.

In the background they could hear the baby giggling and cooing. She wondered at his ability to adapt; even a baby must feel the tension. But Shaan was so good-natured. The absurdity of the situation hit her and she laughed; laughed at Tariq shaking the sugar out of his unkempt hair. She stopped when she saw the expression on his face.

'Throwing things at me? You're tapped!' – pointing a finger to his head – 'I'm your *husband*, remember? The one you must obey!' His shaky finger pointed community verse at her. He did it all the time; everybody did – it was the one thing guaranteed to make her see red, but Tariq didn't seem to know or care. 'You will listen to me!' he yelled. But he was confirming his authority to the air. Saira was gone.

He followed her into the living room. They stood face to face.

'Don't you bloody dare walk out on me! Anybody else would have divorced you by now – I'm the only idiot who'll keep you! The laughing stock of the town! I refuse to be an idiot any longer! I *demand* respect –'

Saira bowed her head. 'Thank you very much for staying married to me. Is that enough or do I have to kiss your feet too?' She bent down as a gesture of feigned obedience.

He slapped her hard across the face.

She stood; he slumped into a corner. Blotches spread over her cheek, her head was ringing with pain. Tariq reached for a magazine and leafed through it. Saira, hurting, wondered what he was waiting for. He turned several more pages, stopped to see what she was doing and then replayed the pattern. She was frozen – the first blow of an evening always froze her – but she managed to glance at her son. Shaan looked up into his mother's eyes. He smiled and chuckled. She smiled back, scooped him up, then Tariq's voice, his intruder's voice, cut in again.

'Is my dinner ready?'

She ignored him. After the blow she would take her time; she knew she would have to cook eventually, but his food wouldn't take priority. She put the baby down on the settee, undressed him and carried him to the kitchen sink. She ran the taps, calmly checking the temperature with her elbow. She heard the mutterings from the living room. Her mind felt ready to explode. She dipped Shaan into the water. He screamed at the unexpected liquid as she washed him quickly.

When she returned, Tariq was sat in front of the television, a stony look to match her own embedded in his face. She placed the baby on the settee, dried him off, applied creams to ease his heat rash. Her husband stared at her. Her body was rigid, ready for a fight, but she feigned relaxation, keeping her skin soft even as the muscles strained.

'When the hell are you going to stop playing mother and get my bloody dinner?'

Cooing gently, she continued to address the baby and its needs.

He paused. She waited to see whether he'd taken the bait. He had no control, she knew this: he knew the game but couldn't resist the challenge. She didn't know why she played along either; only that gentle words from her mouth, any sweetness towards him, would make a mockery of the drudgery she lived.

He got up from his seat and stood tall above her. She looked directly into his eyes. He clenched his fist. She made kissing noises at Shaan as if nothing was bothering her. With great self-control he opened the fist and went back to his seat, knowing the storm was still to come. He banged the remote-control buttons, flicking through the TV channels, trying to find something to watch.

The clock ticked, stretching time like an elastic band. Every moment a vicious battle between two minds. Tariq bit his bottom lip, first gently, then cutting deeper, tasting blood. Saira knew this was war but strode purposefully towards him, handed him the baby and fled into the kitchen for sanctuary. He should take care of his son sometimes. A cold shiver jolted her as she leaned against the kitchen units, trying to organize her chaotic thoughts.

She swiped aside the clutter in the kitchen to make space to prepare the ever-demanding chapattis. Robotic, she turned on the cooker and tried to roll out sheets of sugar paper. The live-in mice had almost completely destroyed the paper and dry flour poured out on to the kitchen surfaces and floor.

She wondered how she could avoid speaking to Tariq during the evening spread out long in front of her; but as soon as she began to think, his shadow – his hands on hips – fell across the small kitchen. She picked up the rolled out chapatti and threw it viciously from side to side. Flour rained across the room. She stole a glance at his face. Neither one of them spoke. She shuffled her feet and moved towards the charred griddle but the stench of burning flour caught in their throats.

Tariq watched her every move, standing in front of her, arms folded. His eyes linked with hers; her unwavering stare forced him to look away. He regained eye contact. This time Saira gave her full attention to the chapattis. Convinced he had won, Tariq tried to laugh but his body was racked by a bout of uncontrollable coughing.

Saira breathed out slowly and threw a chapatti on to the burning griddle. A self-satisfied smirk crossed her tight lips. Tariq saw the expression and moved closer. She stood, ready to fist fight. The second chapatti tore through the middle. He moved closer, intending to teach her a lesson in obedience. She squashed the sticky dough and rolled it back into a ball, seemingly unperturbed. He picked up a glass and filled it with water, leaned into her face. She edged away from him. He smiled at her discomfort. She began to roll out the chapatti again, conscious of the slightest movement. Tariq remained at the sink, a touch away from the cooker.

A mouse crept across the room. Tariq raised his foot and stamped on the creature.

The squealing animal made Saira realize the dangerous game she was playing. Tariq, sneering, watched his wife's face. Saira averted her eyes and carried on with the chapattis. The second chapatti was limp in her hand; the first had burned to a crisp. She kept her eyes focused on a spot in front of her, shoulders sagging.

The mouse lay struggling, guts strewn on the kitchen floor. Tariq's foot came down again. He laughed and grasped hold of Saira's face. Forced to look at him, she rolled her eyes up towards the ceiling.

In the next room Shaan began to cry. They both turned their attention towards the closed door. The kitchen filled with smoke as the unattended chapatti and griddle burned.

Saira looked into the smoke, saw Tariq's devilish face through the black clouds. She wanted to end this power game.

She grabbed hold of the hot griddle and, laughing violently, pushed it towards his face. Tariq stumbled back. She moved forward, he moved backward. The kitchen cupboards all seemed to help. Saira struck him on the side of the head. Raising his hand to his head, he felt clumps of singed hair. Shocked, he lunged forward.

The smoke rose, blocking their lungs. They both coughed and spluttered, but paid no attention to the fire. The battle raged. The cries of the baby in the other room were like minute whimpers as his parents struggled.

Tariq swayed towards her. The smoke was a thick grey sheet, filling the kitchen. Through sheer instinct Saira waved the griddle from side to side. The pan pushed the smoke aside, revealing where she should aim. Tariq cried out in pain. She ignored the cries and carried on hitting. Disorientated by her attack, he arched his back to avoid being burned. The smoke choked both of them, but neither was willing to give up. Saira hit him again, heard the crack of his head against the stove, then a yell of agony. She heard him fall to the ground and, escaping the smoke now, she bumped into his body, trampled over him and pushed the door open.

The baby's cries continued. Saira grabbed him, then hesitated, her head turned towards the kitchen. Behind her, the flames were out of control. The momentary thought gone, she hugged Shaan, picked up her bag and ran.

Flames licked the living-room ceiling, lighting up the thick mass of darkness.

Saira held Shaan close to her breast, shielding him from the heat. They walked through to the front room, which was still calm, the plants and their shadows littering the room. The chasing flames stretched under the door like fingers.

A family of mice piled out of a hole and began to run around, demented. Saira opened the front door and watched the flames come ever nearer. The shadows of the plants stood fast. The mice threw themselves out into the front garden. Saira fell out. In the terraced street a few children played, all else was silent.

She looked up at the house and waited for the black sky to be red once more. Waited for the flames to mount another battle with the night. She opened the back passenger door to the Toyota and shivered as she placed the baby on the seat. She looked back at the house, then slammed the car door. The key to the driver's side jammed in the lock. She ran to the passenger's side, breathless. The baby played contentedly, giggling to himself. Saira fumbled to open the lock. She ran back to the driver's side and jumped in the car. Careful not to rev too much, she kept her lights off and pulled out.

Stopping in a deserted street near by, she waited for the finale. All was silent and dark. Saira watched the sombre black sky above the insignificant terraced houses. A thick

cloud forced itself out of the buildings and began to infilt-
rate the cold air. The flames freed themselves, leaping into
the wind, pushing orange arms through the roof. The baby
watched the gleaming fireworks as they blazed across his
face, smiling as the flames danced in his eyes.

Saira stared out of the windscreen, hypnotized.

Wailing sirens roused her. She watched an ambulance turn
off the Bordesley Green Road into her street, immediately
followed by a fire engine. The drama, live across the sky.
All other senses exhausted, only her eyes were alert. A smile
spread across her lips. Drama played out; the emergency
vehicles drove down the road in silent vigil. Saira got out of
the car. Shaan lay fast asleep. Order had taken over and the
black sky had returned to its original painted state. She
opened the door and gently lifted out the baby. The smell of
burning was strong in the air, threatening to choke her. The
baby awoke and cried. They both coughed. She got back
into the car, the child against her chest. The smell of his
mother calmed him and put him to sleep. Saira held him
tightly in one arm as she clawed off the furry seat covers.
She placed them over her baby. Tired, they fell into a deep
sleep. Later a nightmare forced a shrill scream from her
mouth. *Sirens!* She sat up with a jolt and looked up into the
sky. The sunrise was leaving the world-weary night behind
and she felt uneasy as the sun began to show the secrets
that darkness had hidden.

The nightmare sirens rang in her head. Startled, she shook
herself to banish the noise. The baby woke up and a grubby,
charred woman pushed the hair off her face ready for
another battle.

Fruit Cocktail

James Pogson

I've called him Daddy, Dad and Pops for three decades. It still feels like a title rather than a term of endearment.

I'm supposed to go and see him today; that's the plan. I've got something important I want to ask him, but I'm struggling to come up with the right words. I'm hoping today's the right time and the family home the right place. It's a worry because West Indian men of a certain age are hard to fathom.

My dad's eighty years old. Eighty years old, you know. Bwoy, that's a serious age. The man doesn't look a day over sixty-five. Sometimes I just look at him and think, hey, you've got hair up your nose older than me. Then there are times when I look at him and think I don't know him at all.

He came to this country in 1957, aged thirty-seven. That's quite old to decide you want to begin a new life for yourself in the mother country. You hear stories about why the first generation of West Indian immigrants came to Britain: the economy back home was in a bad state, Britain was crying out for black people to increase its labour force. You've heard those stories. Some planned to come for a five-year stint, to earn enough money and return home. Maybe they didn't think they'd settle, start families and remain for so long.

One day my dad told me his reason. He was a foreman on an estate in St Kitts and they woke him up one night because some of the cattle had escaped from their pen. It was his job to organize the recapture. Standing in his pyjamas at about three in the morning, he thought enough was enough – instructing drowsy men to round up stubborn beasts when you'd been enjoying a sweet sleep minutes before wasn't the best experience in the world – he was going to England. His younger brother had left the island two years before and constantly wrote to him, telling him to do the same. Couldn't be any worse than what he was experiencing right now, and jobs were plentiful apparently. The money was sure to follow in the land of opportunity. Dad says that he'd never worked as hard in his life until he came to Birmingham, England's second city.

It took me thirty years to get that information. Sitting around a kitchen table in St Kitts, Christmas 1999, it just sort of came out in conversation. It felt as if I'd been trying to pick a lock for the longest time, only to find that the door had been on the latch all the while. Despite thirty-eight years of marriage, three sons and a comfortable home in Small Heath, Birmingham, Dad always seemed reluctant to talk about his past. Maybe he was waiting for the right questions to be asked.

I'd nicknamed him 'Don Pogsionni' in St Kitts. The elder statesman. He commands so much love and respect over there. I saw a different side to him, maybe his real side. We built up a kind of respectful rapport during our five-week stay. We've never been there at the same time before, so it was an extraordinary situation to begin with. I remember walking with him and my cousin Larry through his home village one Sunday afternoon, my father between us.

Someone shouted out, 'Me see three man coming, and de youngest one in de middle!' Dad didn't react, but I was laughing. He walked strong and sprightly, despite the arthritis in his spine and his numb feet.

What I remember most are the walks we took through the village, stepping on the dusty grounds where sugar-cane used to flourish, admiring the mountains he used to climb in his youth. Most importantly, we spoke as men, on his terms, on his home ground. It's a feeling I can never quite put into words, nor will I ever forget.

So why is it so damn hard to go round and see him now, a year after our trip? I'm looking out of the window and today's weather forecast is replaying in my head. A sixty per cent chance of rain, cool temperature – about eleven degrees Celsius.

I think Dad and I have always had a problem communicating. When I was a child he used to come home from working at British Leyland in Washwood Heath and utter the immortal words, 'Weh me dinner?' Then, dropping a plastic toy on the floor for me to play with, he'd eat the food that Mom had prepared for him, sit in an armchair in the corner of the living room and fall asleep with the *Evening Mail* over his head. Dad was always around, but not quite, if you know what I mean. Over the years me and my brother William would play a game: see who was able to read the paper and put it back over his head before he'd wake up and ask, 'Anybody wah read de *Evening Mail*?' William, being a boy of mischief and adventure, would flick his ears – they're quite large – without waking him. I can't remember whether I joined in, but it was wickedly funny at the time.

Then there were the times when the front doorbell rang. There'd be a mad scramble. Our instructions were to look through the front-room window first, then shout out who was at the door – well, that bit wasn't part of our instructions – forewarned is forearmed as they say. Dad would pretend that he was watching TV – the black and white one in those days – or reading the same paper that was shielding his eyes from the glare of the light bulb. I was always surprised the front page wasn't printed on his forehead.

He'd sit there casually, man of the house, and entertain in his own way. I could never understand why, when one of his friends came round, he'd develop this amazing interest in what was on TV. I'd sit there, shocked. I didn't believe he could go on so renk, ignore what his mate was saying and give a running commentary about the events unfolding on the screen. Dad did this time and time again. You had to listen carefully to realize that neither of them had a clue what he was on about. Two men, talking at cross-purposes. It reminded me of two people singing different verses of the same song at the same time. The only downside was that each sang a different chorus to a different beat.

Remember the song in *Shaft* about being a complicated man? My dad was like that. What made him tick, boiled his kettle, put the drum in his bass? I remember when they used to refer to Africa as the Dark Continent. That's a good way to describe him. A dark continent of contradictions, mystery, humour, sorrow, watching too much *Oprah Winfrey*, *Jerry Springer* – you name it. Sometimes I'd look into his eyes and just get lost. It was like he was inviting you in, knowing full well that you couldn't suss your way around. In St Kitts I saw pictures of him when he was a much younger man. The eyes were still there, daring you to take a closer look. Back at the house in Small Heath there's a picture of him in the front room; his eyes follow you no matter where you position yourself. In my living room, I've blown up my parents' wedding photograph – the one where they're cutting the cake – laminated it and stuck it on to the wall.

They both more or less look the same today as they did on the fourteenth of July 1962 when they married at Saltley Methodist Church.

My belly's rumbling. Can't go and see Pops on an empty stomach. That's my excuse to hang around a little longer. Don't remember the last time I went out and did a proper shop. As a child I was always told to drink something hot at a time like this, to take the wind out of my seed, or words to that effect. Not in the mood for a drink but a good nyam would fill the gap.

I'm trying hard to think of all the quality time I spent with Dad, growing up. And I've got two pears, four apples, three oranges and a couple of satsumas in the fridge, a pack of mixed vegetables in the freezer compartment, two cartons of semi-skimmed milk and a litre of pure orange juice. Time to do a *McGyver* and make something out of nothing. I don't want to open one of the three tins of tuna or the baked beans in the cupboard. Take the fruit out the fridge; get a plate – nah, a dish, and a sharp knife.

When I used to live at home, it was as if Dad tracked my movements in the kitchen. I'd just begun working for the Civil Service – Department of Trade and Industry, Insolvency Division, dealing with bankruptcies and liquidations. While I was making my breakfast and a packed lunch, Pops would come in and tail me around the room. What the heck was he doing up so early when he didn't have to go anywhere? He'd been retired more than three years by then, but he insisted on getting up and getting in my way. 'You ah go late!' he'd bellow. Oh yeah, and whose fault would that be? Who insisted on going into the bathroom just when I was about to? Who had this urgent desire to do a Delia Smith meets Rusty Lee when I needed to . . . whoa! Easy, calm down. I've been stabbing at the pears and the knife's making a wicked clinking, scraping sound against the base of the enamel dish. Norman Bates eat ya heart out.

I've always found it hard to eat whole fruit. Chewing an apple leaves a bitter taste in my mouth and I have to eat something sweet to counteract the sickly feeling welling up inside. Doesn't that kind of defeat the object? So I think of ways to trick my taste buds and reassure my digestive system that all is well. Mix and match – that's the plan. If I chew and swallow a piece of apple quickly, followed by a slice of orange or a handful of satsuma segments as a disguise, I should be all right. Pity I didn't think of such tactics when I was introduced to Saturday soup.

As children, we dreaded this weekend meal. What was lurking at the bottom of the cooking pot? Pumpkin, sweet potato, green banana, dumplings and the usual suspects – potatoes, carrots, parsnips, chicken. I could take them on their own and in small quantities. It was a different matter when they all ganged up in the one bowl. If the kitchen window was open and the pot lid off, I'd anxiously watch the neighbour's cat in case it accidentally fell in. Years later I acquired a taste for the soup, but back then you had only one choice – eat it or have a stomach full of wind. Sometimes wind felt like the kinder option. Ultimately, when food was dashed – by Dad – or presented – by Mom – on our plates, we had to eat it, plain and simple. The constant reminders of the starving children in Africa were meant to make us feel grateful that we were getting something to eat at all, let alone that day. I remember seeing the same piece of cabbage – complete with distinctive teeth marks – on my plate at least four days in a row. It was a no pain, no gain theory in our house when it came to food.

I'm slicing up the pears, dicing the apples and peeling the satsumas, making a fruit cocktail I can digest. I'm apologizing to my gut in advance, because fruit never fills me up.

I once read that it was best eaten on an empty stomach or in between meals, so I've been trying the eat-fruit-*then*-cook method for the best part of a year. I've got a dish full of the good stuff, a transparent bag filled with the bits I don't want to eat, together with the peelings, plus a knife dripping with fruit juice. I must admit it does look good enough to eat, and it's an excuse not to leave just yet. I'm thinking of Dad again. We can go for days without talking, but he's always in my thoughts. Should I phone him in advance? I expect he'll be in, but wouldn't it be polite to let him know I'm coming?

I have to laugh when I think of him on the phone. He never says hello when he calls, just straight into what he has to say. His conversation starters are, 'You watching de cricket?' or 'You hear de score?' and when I had a car, 'I want you tek me up de road somewhere . . .' It's all very one-sided – he says what he has to say, I react, then it's over – he puts down the receiver. As far as he's concerned, the conversation's done. I know it's goodbye because the line's dead. OK, I know I could try harder to communicate with him, but sometimes the phone calls symbolize our relationship. We talk at each other, not to each other. Except for when we were in St Kitts.

We've both skirted around the issue of the father–son relationship. I'm sure my two older brothers must feel the same way. For me, it's a daunting experience – the isolation and the fear factor. It's a fear of that day of reckoning – the verbal confrontation that may turn nasty because the truth hurts too much. I need to know why he can be so stuck in his ways – St Kitts circa 1920 to 1957. His refusal to answer questions about love, child rearing and parental responsibility. I'm afraid that it will begin a gnawing process, eating away at his soul, making him guilty, angry or oppressed. I'm scared I'll hear and understand the things I've always wanted to. It's the sort of stuff that could make or break our entire relationship.

I don't want to argue and fight, but I do want to know the truth – how much does he love his wife and children, and does he consider himself a good father? There's more, but that's a good starting point. Dad's a man two generations my senior. We come from different worlds, but he's living in mine and I find it hard to tell him he's playing by all the wrong rules, as the quality time we could be spending together disappears for ever. Being scared and angry at the same time can be so frustrating and counterproductive. How can you stop the sands of time from slipping between your fingertips?

I'm taking the fruit into the living room. My Jay Z CD would sound right about now. With the sound at level fifteen, Jay Z begins the introduction to *Volume 3 . . . Life and times of S. Carter* and I'm lounging on my three-seat sofa with a piece of apple between my back teeth. JP listening to Jay Z, moving on to the second track, 'So Ghetto'. Tune! Have to buss this track higher. The fruit's disappearing at a pace to keep up with the rhythm Jay Z's riding. I better be careful, don't want to choke in the process.

I wonder whether Dad realizes today is the anniversary of the death of my godfather, one of his best friends. Ten years ago today we took a train from New Street to Nottingham to pay our last respects to Mr Farrell. We only seem to go to hospital appointments and funerals, Dad and I. Even his younger friends are passing away at a steady rate. I looked at him in the church and imagined how I'd feel if he was lying in the casket instead. As children we used to joke that he slept in his armchair as if he were 'tone mudda dead', to steal a phrase from my parents. I always feel particularly close to Dad at funerals, but I never talk to him about it. Perhaps because I heard him cry for the first and only time at Aunt Emelda's funeral in St Kitts. He was sitting directly behind me, but I didn't have the heart to turn around and see for myself.

Today I woke up feeling as if I'd burst if I didn't confront him. There was a pounding sensation travelling through my chest, but now it feels like a distant tremor. I feel guilty trying to suppress the emotion, but what the hell *do* you do with the pain?

When it comes to hip-hop I make a point of listening to the lyrical content. It's not just about the beats and sensational rhymes for me. Eyes closed, eating fruit, I'm picturing myself standing next to Pops. We're both dressed in suits, looking straight ahead. He's in me and a piece of me is in him. I have his height, his forehead, his knees – thanks, Dad – and his stubborn streak. I stopped arguing with him years ago. Mentally, I agreed to disagree because arguing had stopped serving a purpose. He never says sorry when he's wrong, but why should he? Somehow my picture's turned into a rap video where we're acting out some sort of gangsta scenario. Dad's sitting down, he's the Don. I'm his lieutenant. Scratch that. I blame Jay Z.

I'm still afraid to talk to my dad. Frightened to ask him why he's always left the upbringing of his three sons to his wife, our mother. Pops, your then twenty-year-old bride, now a woman approaching retirement age, taught me how to play cricket, how to pitch marbles and spoke about her childhood and life experiences. She's lived with you all these years and still goes out to work each day. I want to know your story, Dad, but a big part of me is afraid to ask. That's what today's about, because I don't want to remember you as an absent father. Absent not in body, but in spirit. Is your behaviour based on your own upbringing? Did you apply the five-point plan to women – cook, clean, wash, iron and breed? Are you like the farmer who scatters his seed across the land, expecting nature to take its course and then accepting all the credit when the crops grow in abundance without any real effort on his part?

The last slice of apple's disappearing down my throat. There's a piece of pear left in the dish. I imagine I've left the best piece till last. Jay Z is 'Big Pimpin' – track eleven – and my eyelids feel heavy. It's raining hard now. The music drowns out the patter against the window, but the clouds are welling up in that angry, grey, vexing fashion which tells you that it isn't gonna go away anytime soon.

The pear slice is what's left of my fruit cocktail. I'm right, it's the sweetest piece of all. There's a message in here somewhere, isn't there? The contents of my dish – all the good and bad stuff mixed up to produce a palatable concoction. The bitter and the sweet. Isn't that what life's all about? One big dose, one potent cocktail – and it goes down the same way.

I don't like getting wet and I try to avoid confrontations. Pops never knew I was coming anyway. What's the old saying? 'What you don't know won't hurt you.' That's not always true – it's what I don't know that's tearing my insides apart. I know that deep in his heart Dad loves me and I have to admit I love him too, but we've never told each other so. Now I think of other sayings I grew up with. 'When you dig ditch, dig two; one for me and one for you.' 'God nah sleep.' 'Fowl who sleep a roost, ain't too hard to catch.' There are loads of them and they all make me smile, but one in particular reminds me of my current situation – 'Wha you buy you wear.' You must always take responsibility for your actions. Whatever you decide to do, you must live with the consequences.

Jay Z's gone and Natalie Cole is singing. I'm standing quite still. Natalie's tribute album to her father, Nat King

Cole, is one of my favourites. This track has a soothing, haunting melody which I really love. I can hear those voices vibrating against my ribcage. My heart's a speaker with way too much bass. I raise an imaginary glass, silently toasting my father.

The rain pours off my leather baseball cap on to the lower part of my coat, then bounces beneath my heavy-duty boots.

Mobile phone sheltered in my inside pocket.

I'm dreading the walk up Green Lane, not because it's raining but because of everything else that will follow.

But this is it.

I punch two digits to access a number from its memory, then hear a familiar voice on the end of my mobile. Time to ask some questions.

'Hi, Dad, it's me.'

The Hijab

Ava Ming

Closing the garden gate behind her, she adjusted her hijab
to form a snug fit against the chilly wind. The black material stretched around her face and down past her shoulders,
ensuring her head and neck were completely covered. Next,
a brief tug on each finger of the black gloves that added
sophistication to the hijab and matching long black cloak
while hiding unkempt nails. *Subhan-allah, alhamdu-lillah,
allahu-akbar. Glory to God, Thank you God, God is great.* A
familiar mantra whispered as she gathered pace along the
road.

The hijab, which covered her hair whenever she left the
house, was as familiar to her as dreadlocks to a Rastafarian
or a sari to an Indian woman. But still she knew that people
would find it hard to disguise their surprise at seeing a black
woman in such clothing. She didn't think she would ever
get used to the stares and glances which made her feel self-
conscious and uncomfortably unique. *I wear this clothing to
please you, Oh Allah, please don't let anybody stare today . . .*

She breathed deeper as the hill inclined; a Jeep pulling
into the corner petrol station triggered thoughts of yesterday's

encounter at the garage. The mechanic had called her 'little lady' as he detailed the many faults on her old car. It was only when she mentioned the pertinent phrase, 'my husband', that any level of respect for her became apparent. When she was ready to drive out of the MOT-testing centre he had regarded her curiously before finally blurting out:

'What nationality are you?'

Here we go again. Inwardly annoyed but outwardly calm – *That's my face and I like it smooth*, her husband always said – she'd responded without emotion.

'What do you mean?'

'Well.' He pointed to the Islamic sticker on the dashboard – Arabic lettering on a bright green background – and gestured at her Muslim hijab. 'Are you Iranian or Libyan? I mean, you must be Egyptian or something!'

Relishing the thought of bursting his bubble, but also feeling slightly mean she replied, 'My parents are from Jamaica!'

He was both crushed and surprised. 'Well, I'd never have guessed!'

Who cares what you'd have guessed, why should I wear a label to keep you happy?

She was almost there. Her breathing eased as she walked a little slower, the crest of the hill finally under her feet. The sights, sounds and atmosphere of the Soho Road, Handsworth, all in view. On her left were the remnants of the outdoor market – only two traders remained. The dark entrance doors of the post office concealed long queues of benefit claimants. Shopkeepers carrying bulging bags of change hurried in; pensioners paid the weekly fiver on their TV licences. Brightly dressed refugees from Kosovo or somewhere, a new addition to the area, wrapped their babies in chest slings and comforted their older children who seemed bewildered by the strangeness of this new world.

Leaving the car at home had been a good idea. The brisk walk energized her. For a while she'd been eighteen again, two stone slimmer, with twice the attitude. But no hijab. Islam was not a faith she'd grown up in. It had been a conscious choice made a little over a year ago. Now she couldn't imagine going out with her head uncovered and not living according to the rules of Islam. To her it was more than just a religion, it was a blessed way of life.

As a teenager she'd been popular and well mannered, but her parents had assumed it was only a matter of time before she became reckless, inconsiderate and challenging. Perhaps it would have made their lives more interesting, but even twenty years ago she'd refused to wear the labels assigned to her. Instead she'd done well at school and university. She hadn't become pregnant during her student days and had gained a reputation for being ready to assist friends in need. Sometimes she'd been warned that she was too nice, in danger of being taken for granted. But if being nice was a flaw then she'd learned to live with it. Now she wore her hijab and long outer cloak to express her reversion to Islam, seen by Muslims as the religion of all mankind. She called it reversion because the Quran taught that all people were Muslims simply because God or Allah had chosen for them to be born.

Soho Road. Vibrant, energetic, Eastern, Caribbean, scents, noise, old people, young mothers, teenagers, children, traffic, businessmen and most of all, colour. In the mid-1980s Handsworth was infamous because of the riots. Now it had evolved into a miniature Punjab. Instead of Tesco there was Rehmans Supermarket, where there had been Dorothy Perkins there was Sahota Boutique. There were five halal butcher shops along the length of the road, intermingled with sweet shops, grocers, the technical college and the library, both preserved as listed buildings. More recently, an explosion of beauty parlours had sprung up – offering cures for every type of ugliness. Soho Road had a reputation for fashion innovation. A profusion of shops selling material encouraged the buyer to wander from one to the next, drifting away a whole afternoon running silk through fingers, holding velvet naps, mixing and matching patterns and plains, the rough against the smooth, satin and brocade, filling an imaginary wardrobe with glamorous pieces.

'Yo sister!'

A loud shout from a man leaning on the door of the pub startled her out of her reverie. She was still standing in the middle of the street and was getting blown about by the increasingly harsh October wind. Now she'd got here she wasn't sure which direction to go in. As she focused on the man in the doorway she realized that it was happening again. Despite her fervently whispered *dua*, her prayer as she had set out on her walk, people were staring. *Yar Allah, please make them look away . . .*

The hijab and cloak were supposed to make her blend in, reduce the chances of drawing attention to herself. But in reality they seemed to do just the opposite. Perhaps it was time she wore a veil that left only her eyes uncovered and allowed her to make secret faces at all the starers.

Why did people have to be so obvious? Was she the only person who knew how to glance discreetly at someone else? Nosiness was understandable, if not acceptable. It seemed that most people were born nosy and then conditioned to believe in labels: all brown-skinned people with long thick hair were Asians from India or Pakistan with singsong accents, they ate spicy foods and celebrated Divali. All black people came from Jamaica, were called West Indians and loved sunshine and reggae music. Irish people were lazy, Jews had big noses and curly dark hair, and white people? Well they were simply there to guide everyone else in the right, white way. Labels. Ridiculously stereotyped labels. Now here she was confusing people so much they had no choice but to stare.

How long would it be until someone approached her? Might as well start counting. One . . . two . . . three . . . she knew it was coming. Stares on every side. She told herself to just keep walking. One foot in front of the other. Thirty-two . . . thirty-three . . . thirty-four . . . she approached the biggest material shop on the Soho Road. Peace and sanctuary? She hoped so. Seventy-nine . . . eighty . . . eighty-one . . . if she could just make it to one hundred. Perhaps today could be a probe-free day. She opened the door, stepped into the shop, smiled at the assistants, walked over to the bolts of material. Ninety-seven . . . ninety-eight . . . *Doing well, so far so good.*

'Excuse me!'

Almost made it! A gentle tap on the back of her shoulder and an unfamiliar voice made her turn round slowly. She faced an attractive, slender woman of about twenty-five with wispy black shoulder-length hair, wearing a long beige coat over a woollen sweater and black trousers. Chic black suede boots completed the outfit. The young woman was accompanied by an older lady with light brown eyes enlarged by thick spectacle lenses. This woman was dressed in a brightly patterned sari, what looked like a Marks & Spencer's cardigan and comfy shoes. Her grey hair was pinned up in a bun. The two women looked at her, smiling nervously. That's when she noticed the eyes of the younger woman. Deep brown, almond shaped, expressive and sincere. The perfectly manicured hand that had tapped on her shoulder now gestured towards her; rose-painted lips completed the picture.

'I don't mean to be rude but my mother and I saw you outside wearing that beautiful hijab. Are you a Muslim?'

She felt annoyed but stayed silent, wondering why the old lady had begun to clutch her arm. *Smile graciously at the*

191

nosy woman and her mother. Scroll through the prepared answers filed in your memory. Choice 1: Do you know you're the fifth person to ask me that in two days? Choice 2: What business is it of yours and why are you bothered? Choice 3: Who do you intend to pass this bit of gossip on to? Close friends and family or a whole community? Choice 4: How would you feel if a complete stranger asked you about your religion?

She decided to reject all those responses and be nice. After all, the woman had said it was a beautiful hijab.

'My name is Aisha and yes, I am a Muslim.'

'I thought so,' the young woman continued. 'I don't mean to pry but you see so few black Muslims. Is it OK to call you black? You're not from Morocco or something are you?'

The gracious smile froze into place; she didn't know what to say in response. *Why is your mother still holding my arm? Wish you'd go away and take your mother with you.*

The daughter started to explain. 'You see, we're Sikhs, but my sister recently married a Muslim. He's, well, he's black . . .'

Smile and nod, smile and nod. What do they want from me?

'The marriage was a great surprise,' she went on. 'You know, we just assumed she'd marry a Sikh. One of her own. She's very pretty, got a good education, great job, but for some reason she married a Muslim. Abdullah his name is. Almost broke my mother's heart.'

Still smiling, still nodding, starting to feel like one of those puppy-dog toys in the back of some cars.

'Is your mother upset because he's Muslim or because he's black?'

Oops. Big oops. I'd only meant to think that question, not ask it out loud.

Now it was their turn to look embarrassed. The older woman who had been silently looking at her throughout the conversation seemed to grip her arm even tighter. What exactly did they want from her, for goodness' sake? Did they think this Abdullah was her brother or something? What did they expect her to say?

'You don't understand. My mother just wants to talk to you. She doesn't know anything about being a Muslim. She wants to know what it's like for my sister, perhaps find a way to become close again. Will you talk to us, please?'

What could she do? How to respond? No need to smile graciously any more, things had suddenly become serious. Had her hijab somehow made her a spokesperson for black Muslims? What could she say to these people to reassure them without compromise, without sounding patronizing? Islam was a glorious faith but to them it had become a source of pain, possibly embarrassment. How could she speak for Abdullah when she didn't even know him? How could she build a bridge for them without knowing how wide, how high, what length to begin to construct it? *Oh Allah, if this is a test please don't let me take it by myself.*

The young woman continued to talk while ushering Aisha towards the door of the shop and out on to the street. Confused, she assumed they would stop and arrange a time to meet but instead they pulled her along with increasing urgency. With one on each arm she secretly named them Teena and Meena until she could ask their real names. They made their way through crowds, across busy roads, squeezed between pushchairs and shoppers. No time for her to say, *What's happening? Hold on, where are we going? What's the rush?*

People stopped at the sight of a black Muslim woman being escorted briskly through Handsworth in such a manner. Meanwhile, Teena chatted on about how she would be a great help to them and Meena wordlessly squeezed her arm. *Where are they taking me?* They turned one corner, then another, zipped past more shops and people until finally they approached the Sikh Gurdwara. A Sikh temple! Her mind reeled at the thought. What would a Muslim do in a Sikh temple?

The bright orange and white of the exterior walls loomed in front of her. Cars lined the tarmac. Words in unfamiliar lettering were painted on the walls. Words eluded her as she struggled to process what was happening. Had she consented to go with them? Hadn't she just gone out to look at some material, buy some chocolate and then go home? After too many hours spent inside the house, fresh air and a walk had seemed like a good idea, but a devious kidnapping to a Sikh temple? Unsurprisingly, the thought had never entered her mind!

Had this ever happened before: a Muslim in a Sikh temple? How would the worshippers react to her? What would be expected of her? Should she remove her head-covering? Did men and women pray together, or separately as in a mosque? Would she be asked to sit through a ceremony before Meena and Teena spoke to her? Would they offer food? Would it be halal? Too shocked to speak, the myriad of questions rose in her mind as she was pulled into the building. It was her smiling and nodding that had done it. She'd thought she was being accommodating and polite. They'd obviously mistaken her gestures for acquiescence. But when had they actually said, 'Let's go to the temple and talk'? That suggestion alone would have stopped her nodding and smiling for a very long time!

The pressure on her arms had subsided. The constant noise of Teena's pleas also stopped. Small groups of people spoke in quiet tones around them. There was calm, there was peace. They were in the Gurdwara. Both women seemed immediately at home. Good for them. She, however, did not know what to do with herself. Stay standing or take a seat? Kick off her shoes or leave them on? Smile generally around the room or avoid eye contact? Run back through the door to freedom or stand there like an idiot?

Now it seemed that the pockets of people dotted around the large entrance hall were becoming aware of her. Some smiling, some curious. Some venturing a 'Hello, how are you today?' as they walked past. A group of older women came closer, taking in her hijab and cloak and asking where she had acquired them. Meena and Teena began to greet people they knew, gradually loosening their grip and leaving her side.

Even as she began to relax, she was aware that she stood out. Everyone else was of South Asian descent. The men clothed in business suits and turbans. The women wrapped in beautiful saris and some of the younger ones, like Teena, dressed in Western clothes. She was black, dressed all in black, a female, a Muslim in a hijab. Could she have stuck out any more? But what did they want from her? How long would they keep her here? She had no idea what to expect. Vaguely remembered television images of Gurdwara weddings and ceremonies gave no clue as to why she was here.

A tall man with a distinguished greying beard, dark suit and expensive shiny black shoes strode across the hall. He stood directly in front of her and smiled a welcome.

'Good afternoon.'

Good afternoon? Were they expecting her? Hadn't he noticed she was Muslim? Seeing the bewildered look in her eyes, the man began to laugh.

'My name is Mr Kumar and I am the manager of this temple. Welcome to the Gurunanak Gurdwara. Don't worry, you're not late. The ladies have just finished preparing lunch. You are staying for lunch, aren't you? Allow me to take you through. I think a small crowd's gathering.'

A small crowd? Gathering! Take her through! What was going on? And why had Meena and Teena apparently evaporated, leaving her to her fate?

Mr Kumar's voice was gentle as he ushered her across the hall and through a door into a medium-sized room.

'I know everyone here's looking forward to hearing you speak . . .'

Speak?

'We had a very interesting Christian lady last week,' he said. 'Next week we're expecting a lady from the Quaker Society, but we've never had a black Muslim before. I think I'll sit in on your talk myself. I'm quite looking forward to hearing it. By the way, shall I introduce you as Nation of Islam or traditional Muslim?'

Aisha closed her eyes, shaking her head slightly as the reality of her circumstances became clear to her. When she opened them again she saw a sea of smiling faces, a swathe of colourful saris, long hair, hair pinned up, grey hair, black hair. Some faces with glasses, some with make-up on, some without. Old women, young women, women nursing babies and in the midst of all this, the co-conspirators Meena and Teena. Their previous anxiety had all gone, in its place the smug satisfaction of a job well done. *A job well done . . .* Pondering slowly over these words, she realized she'd been tricked! Sucked in by their worried and pitiful pleas on behalf of their sister. She had to admit they were good, very good. How often did they do this? Every week? Despite her predicament she couldn't help but laugh out loud in disbelief.

Noticing her tension disappear, Mr Kumar turned to her and joked, 'Don't worry we don't expect you to read the Guru Granth Sahib, our holy book, on your first visit.' Turning to the seated crowd he went on: 'Good afternoon, ladies, welcome to our Thursday meeting. We'd like to thank Sanjeet and her mother Mrs Bansal for once again finding us a guest speaker for today.'

She was right: they had done this before.

'As you can see our guest today is a Muslim. Her name is Aisha and now she'll talk to you for a while about her faith, after which we'll share some lunch downstairs. I'm sure you'll all do your best to make her feel at home this afternoon.'

Warm applause followed Mr Kumar's introduction. She was still the centre of attention but how different it felt to the stares out on the street. It wouldn't take long – half an hour, an hour at the most. All she had to do was relax, be herself, talk and maybe answer a few questions. No problem.

Slipping off her shoes and sitting down, she gave a bright smile. She winked at the mischievous Meena and Teena, then with a slow, deep breath she began.

'My name is Aisha and I am proud to be a follower of Islam.'

A Solitary Dance

Naylah Ahmed

I hate the photograph. It so completely explodes the myth of 'Asian princess meets Mogul prince' that it grates on me. None of the pictures taken at my parents' wedding evoke images of the Taj Mahal, those romantic days when people sacrificed their lives for love.

Description: a girl – my mother – sits, head lowered, hands folded over her bent knees. She keeps to tradition, anticipating the arrival of her groom nervously. No upward glance, no hint of excitement – more a downward, reflective look at the feet of the guests admiring her bridal gown. She is the centrepiece, in a gown as red as a ripe tomato, embroidered with threads of gold which map a meandering journey across the delicate fabric. A journey she would take months later, to a place where the red stays on tomatoes and delicate fabrics become weather-beaten in a moment of rain.

The image sits lopsided in its frame, staring back at me from above the fireplace. How strange to think it's been here, seen by no one, during the months my mother was in hospital. I wonder if the bride lifts her veil and peers out at the living room when no eyes are watching her. What would she see? These caramel-glazed, smoke-stained walls, like the ageing wedding image itself.

What is that smell? It's been irritating my nostrils since I entered the house; its familiarity takes me to the blurry edges of memory. A childhood smell.

Perhaps I should leave. There is nothing for me here.

The smell is getting stronger. Recognition bursts my bubble and the smell escapes, causing my stomach to fall with a wet slap.

Urine.

I can't move to the front door. My bladder throbs faintly. I look up at that familiar spot on the staircase and am almost sure I hear it creak under the weight of a girl who once spent hours there. I think I see her, somewhere between a memory and my reflection in the hall mirror; I see her and I know what she's thinking. There is movement in the living room – but the door is wide open and the room was empty a moment ago . . .

I'm standing on the stairs and I need to pee. I'm sure I've already been, not too long ago, but there's a burning in my bladder and I really, really need to go again . . . but I'll hold it.

Normally I'd go straight downstairs, through the kitchen and into the loo, but then today isn't normal, is it? They're shouting – but no matter how loud they shout I can't make out what they're saying. All I can hear is 'I HATE YOU, I HATE YOU' over and over again, because that's what they mean, isn't it?

The burning is getting worse, but so is the shouting. I can't walk past and pretend I don't hear them. What would they do if I stopped in the middle of the room? What would I do?

The answer is so simple now. They would have continued arguing. I could never admit, back then, that had I walked into that room with my hair alight, singing Diana Ross's

'Chain Reaction' they wouldn't have batted an eyelid. So there I was, stuck halfway up or down the stairs – depending on where I was going and where I was coming from, I could never remember – with sweaty, empty hands and a bladder fit to burst. Then it would come. As those words grew louder and louder in my head – *'I hate you, I hate you, I hate YOU'* – drowning out the shouting, I would suddenly be faced by a constricting silence. A silence that would wrap itself around me until all I could feel was the hypnotic thump of my own heartbeat.

I hear it now: the moist, uncomfortable quiet of unspoken words. It's like peeing your pants and then standing still in a hot room; the scent of urine muzzled by the heat, silently expanding to reach every corner, vague but present. Their anger used to expand in silence.

She's moved to the kitchen now and the pots and pans are screaming as she bangs them from worktop to cupboard and back again. She likes the way the banging interrupts the silence, his silence. I can smell his cigarette breath as he speaks his soundless thoughts. They make a smoky alphabet that yawns into the hallway and up the stairs. Why can I still hear them? They finished and went their separate ways a few moments ago: her to the kitchen, him to the lounge. The tape recorder is playing again.

Arguing should be banned.

There was a tedium in my parents' arguments that was torturous. Even when they paused my mental tape-recordings would fill in the gaps, no matter what I was doing at the time. It was so easy to remember, always the same things said in the same order – as if on cue. I would stand out of sight, ready to prompt if one of them missed a line. It was as if I had spent my childhood listening to the same irritating song over and over. After a time their voices were of no consequence; their whispers and yells had the consistency of corrugated iron, monotonous.

I still hear their voices. They exclude me, of course – that part remains unchanged – but they argue on, despite my new surroundings. They are with me somehow.

I move back to the living room. It's safer here, in their space, because I know that they've gone for good. Now their space is a comfortable no-man's land where I'm free. No matter what I hear or see or smell, they've gone. Two grey gravestones cement their absence. But I'm here. I'm still the stranger they lived with, in my floral dresses and pretty girl's clothes, enveloped in the smell of faded urine and cigarette smoke, dancing on the stairs.

This time they're upset about the car. It sits on our drive, clean and shiny, unaware that it's the cause of so much hatred. They think they're doing the grown-up thing by taking turns to drive the car to work – but grown-ups can't share. They're too big and selfish. Adults find it hard to watch someone else enjoy something while waiting for their turn. But I'm glad they share. I'm glad because I was the problem before the car came.

They hate collecting me from school, but I can never tell them what it's like for me – waiting outside the classroom until even the teachers are ready to go home – and they keep battling in silence, happy to pretend that it's not their turn to pick me up. I don't look at the teachers any more because there's no sympathy in their eyes. They're just angry because they have to wait.

I remember the day they both turned up: her on the bus and him in the car.

She'd held out quite some time, convinced it should be his turn because he had the car. He'd collected me several times that week and wanted her to do it for once. They didn't see the teachers – didn't even thank them. Nor did they

201

notice the damp eyes of the quiet girl they'd come to collect. All they saw was their dispute in a uniform.

I wish I could cry, but I won't – not even when it gets really bad. I guess because it's not about me at all. It's about what happened before me. There is a 'them' that exists without me. I will always be the enemy when they're fighting. He says I'll grow up to be just like her and make demands on some 'poor soul' in his shoes. And she always sees me like him, needing more of her time, eating away at her twenty-four hours a day.

The funny thing is that they reminded me of each other. Even their faces were similar: they both wore the same frown, had the same cross lines etched on their foreheads. Masculinity and femininity found a marriage in their countenances.

You should cry – I still can't.

The jingle of keys is a bad sign. It means he's mad enough to leave the house. When he leaves what shall I do? What will she do?

She'd murder porcelain while he took the car and sucked down roads like spaghetti, and nothing was resolved. People say that time heals everything – and it does, but is that right? How much time? The saying never helped me – waiting for them to speak took an eternity. How does a person live between eternities of silence? I could tell you. I have lived one on this very staircase.

The phone is ringing and the pans stop bumping into one another for a moment. She's in the hallway, her lungs like full balloons, about to shout my name, hoping it might reach under my door and through my headphones. But I'm not in my room. I'm standing on these stairs, waiting for her to spot a corner of my dress in the shadows. The phone has stopped ringing. Perhaps the phone was afraid of being banged about like the pots and pans and decided not to interrupt her. She's gone back into the kitchen now, I can hear her. She didn't call me. I wish she'd called me.

I have to be quiet now . . .

That familiar feeling of being out of place, a stranger in my own home. In the old days, when they were fighting, everything I touched spoke louder than it did normally. When I sneaked back to my room giveaway floorboards would squeak and creak like dying animals, trying to get their attention. But they never did notice. Not once did they stop between hisses or yells to come and see who was on the other side of the living-room door. So I became a silent shadow moving in accordance with their angry sun. An inseparable part of them, never acknowledged, always behind them, stretched or shrunken by the force of their frustrations.

I feel love and hate, and somewhere in between those two emotions sits indifference. I stand once again at that indecisive point in the belly of the staircase, five stairs from the top. Here I would see and not be seen, hear and not be heard. But standing here now there is nothing to see, nothing to hear. These floorboards, which once seemed like screaming animals facing death, now squeak mouse-like, barely audible. In the spaces created by my parents' absence I grow and fill this empty place – with *me*. The silence invites me to breathe.

When he left for good she was wailing at him again – only this time her eyes were wet and his ears heard nothing. His final send-off was torn by her shrieks of displeasure, mimicking the send-off he had faced at the start of every working day throughout their marriage. I looked at her and wondered whether time really was a healer. In all the years they'd spent together she had never been pleased and he had never been content. But when I looked down at his waxy face in the coffin I caught a glimpse of something that resembled contentment.

His blue ears were muffled by lank hair in that airless box, protecting him from her wails.

Somewhere, under two mounds of soil, inside wooden boxes, they lie silent. Both in pristine white garb, both with a smooth brow – side by side. Is he free of the sound of her? I don't think so, somehow.

I should leave. There really is nothing here for me now.

The red of the bridal gown in the picture is the only happy thing in this room. That vibrant red, so distinct from the empty white she was buried in. Maybe I don't hate the photograph, this one last piece of my parentage. In this lop-sided image *they* are the grey mass of indifference lying between my extremes of love and hate, holding their breath. This single picture captures their existence without their inseparable shadow. Here they can see and not be seen, hear and not be heard; my father's presence implied by the occasion, my mother's unseen countenance bowing, indifferent, under the heavy, ornate gown.

I move to the front door, stopping only to glance at two shadows dancing on the stairs. Outside it is a warm day; my shadow stretches, giant-like, across the lawn.

Secret Life
Kwa'mboka

Once upon a time, there was a beautiful young single mother. This woman-child, called Venus, was just eighteen years old and had one beloved daughter. It was 1960, just before Independence, so the East African country she lived in was still legally segregated. There were separate suburbs for Africans, Europeans and Asians; separate schools and doctors. There were services and courtesies available for Europeans which were not extended to Asians and certainly not dreamed of by most Africans, especially young, unmarried native mothers.

One cold July evening – July being the coldest month of the year – Venus's baby suffered convulsions. Neighbours drove them to the Asian hospital, money changed hands and the child was admitted. They called the paediatrician, who arrived within the hour. He was a tall, handsome, pale-bronze man, with wavy gold hair, who smelled of cigars and whiskey. He gently examined the baby girl. He smiled at Venus in the hesitant manner of one wishing to reassure without giving false hope. The doctor's name was Adam Harris. He gave rapid instructions, then took Venus aside.

Dr Harris explained in simple, slow English that he thought the baby had meningitis. Venus had to be strong, he said, looking her in the eye.

The Ingereza didn't normally explain themselves or look natives in the eye. They did not hold one's elbow gently or carefully rock African babies after an examination. Venus watched the doctor leave the ward.

Five hours later, the Hindu nurse called an Anglican priest to pray for the child. Dr Harris came back after the priest had gone, smiling vaguely at Venus before bowing his sleep-tousled head over the child's cot. Venus and the doctor watched the baby sleep through the night. By midday the child was smiling, alert and hungry. A miracle. Venus sparkled and smiled at everyone. The world was good, God was merciful and the doctor had been so kind.

Dr Harris insisted that Venus bring the child to his surgery the next day. He looked after the girl child with a tenderness and attention that astounded the young African mother. Harris began to call at their one-room apartment with gifts for Venus and trinkets for the child. He seemed content to watch the child play and to make Venus laugh, revealing the gap between her front teeth. He spoke little, but spent hours watching them or sometimes reading from a foreign newspaper. Venus, the baby and the neighbours got used to his visits. They called Harris 'Daktari', Kiswahili for doctor. Daktari began to share their simple evening meals and to bring them provisions, medicines and even new clothes on his visits.

Venus had no dealings with men. She did not want any more children and sex with men led to children. Men had meant nothing but painful, violent, abusive encounters until she met Daktari. She did not understand his ways, but she felt safe and was grateful for his silent friendship.

Eighteen months passed in this quiet, sweet way, then

one Sunday morning, just after the crack of dawn, Daktari knocked on the window. Venus unbolted the wooden door and watched him stumble into the sleeping room, bringing with him the stench of beer, cigarettes and angry fear. He had not visited for a fortnight and had not washed or slept for most of that time. He lurched into her arms and they fell on to the single bed, all the while Daktari mumbled, 'This I cannot do, this I cannot be.'

Fully awake, slightly fearful, but determined not to disturb the baby, Venus rolled Daktari to one side, humming a lullaby so the baby would not wake. The white man stopped mumbling and fell into a restless slumber. She removed his shoes, socks and shirt, covered him with her single sheet and stirred the charcoal embers in her morning fire. The baby woke up smiling and chattering. Venus picked her up and started to feed her. Daktari stirred and sat up for a few moments, watching them. Venus smiled at him and carried on with her Sunday tasks until he slept again. At midday a neighbour took the baby for a walk, leaving Venus in her room with the sleeping Harris. Venus stood by the bed, looking at him. At his features, his large frame, his skin which was very white wherever the sun had not touched it. She reached across to feel his yellow hair.

His hand shot up, clasping her wrist.

'You have no idea what you've put me through since I first met you. You with your simple ways, your uncomplicated life, your beautiful smile. Perhaps you know exactly what you do to me. Perhaps you are just like the whores in the bars – a tease, a manipulative jungle bitch. They all want it – don't even have to pay them. You all want it, don't you, you little chocolate fuck-bunnies? Well, today I'm going to give it to you. I thought you were different but you're not. You can't be. "Fuck her and be done with it," Eversham's been saying for months. I thought I loved you, that I would find a way to love you in this godforsaken country, but he's right. This feeling cannot be. If I fuck you now, it will stop my fantasies. I won't feel anything, I'll be free of you, I will never have to see you again.'

Venus twisted about on the pivot of her captive wrist. She did not fully understand his words but his eyes, his breath, the baring of his teeth terrified her. Now Daktari looked like the three men who had once followed her from the bus-stop, down the narrow path to her mother's home in their village. She'd known the men as childhood companions, but on that day, at dusk, they'd suddenly become her enemies. Taunting her with jibes about her ironed town hair, her spike-heeled town shoes, her big town job. At first, she had not been afraid and answered back, taunt for taunt, thinking this was a strange game. Then they blocked her path and hissed the language of conquest, envy and power-lessness.

One pulled out his flaccid penis and shouted at the other two to hold her down as he frantically pulled his foreskin back and forth. Pinned to the red earth of the path, gripped by the reality of the situation, tears of anger and bewilder-ment rolled out of the corners of Venus's eyes. The men saw the tears and became hard, erect. The more she cried, the larger each penis grew, until one by one each shoved himself into her, pounded into her, withdrew from her and spat on her.

'Town whore, we were the first in you, dirty town cunt!' Her childhood playmates hissed in triumph as they cleaned blood off their members with leaves and shirt-tails before running into the darkness of the village night. Venus did not know which one was the father of her child.

Dr Harris held on to her wrist with one hand and pulled out his pappy penis with the other. He continued to speak, looking at her, but not seeing her. She stared at the vivid pink of his manhood, astounded. It was the same shape as those of African men and it was more or less the same size, but it was not growing. She wanted to laugh at her discovery. They were all alike.

She giggled. He slapped her face. Tears rose and involuntarily slid down her cheeks. She began to whimper. He stopped.

'I am sorry, I am so sorry. I don't know what to do. I can't go on like this, do you even understand?'

He kneeled on the bed, exposed, trying to hold her, to comfort her, to comfort himself. She stopped struggling and slumped against him. He looked into her vacant eyes. She saw nothing. Venus had left her body, refusing any part of this familiar nightmare. He pulled her on to the bed, all the time stroking and caressing her. She did not resist, did not comply. He sucked the milk from her still-rounded breasts. She did not move, did not even sigh. He stroked and scratched her amber thighs. They did not part; they did not press together. He ran a forefinger from her anus to her clitoris. She was not wet, nor unusually dry. He rolled on top of her and placed his penis at the mouth of her vagina.

Her unseeing eyes looked into his face.

'You are so beautiful, you are so tight, oh God, I love being inside you. Do you like it? Am I doing well? Is doctor making it better? Is doctor making it all better? Is doctor . . . ahhh.'

Venus lay deathly still. She had left her body under Harris; gone away. He pulled out of her, kissed her closed eyelids, her pert nipples, her stomach, and slipped his tongue into the groove between her legs, licking and sucking his deed away, licking and sucking his silent goddess until a wave ran through her body, rocking her, rocking him.

Dr Harris loved Venus. He did not understand he had raped her. He did not know that each time he came to her he raped her. Venus did not fight; she did not refuse. Men, she assumed, always took women in this way, without asking. At least Daktari no longer hit her, nor did he have to see her cry to grow. She sent the baby to a neighbour when he called. At dawn, she collected the baby for her morning feed. In this way, Harris could still enjoy the innocence of the woman-child and her baby, and his heart turned painfully in his chest with a love and a yearning he could not bear.

They were lying on her bed; Venus far away in a place he could not reach, Daktari leaning on his elbow, stroking and watching. *She's pregnant*, he thought calmly. He saw it in the rise of her breasts, touched it in the hardness of her small round belly.

'This I cannot do, this I cannot be,' he muttered.

He pulled on his clothes and slammed out of her life.

Venus gave birth to a milky white male child with blue-green eyes and straight brown hair. The scandalized hospital staff passed the fair child from crooked arm to arm whispering, gurgling, examining and casting Venus the evil eye. Venus's mother called her a white man's whore; her neighbours smiled and called the child 'Boy'. Dr Harris saw his son at six weeks. He held the child to him. He walked around his office with the boy in his arms. He spoke and cried into the baby's blanket. In time, he gave the boy back to Venus.

'Stay away from me. Both of you, you and that bastard half-caste of yours. Stay away from me, understand?'

Venus left the surgery suffocating herself and the child with anger. Boy started crying, his eyes wide with fear. On the bus his cries turned into furious high-pitched screams as his mother turned him this way and that, eventually pinching him into silence.

That night, Venus's milk dried up and two small lines

appeared at the corners of her mouth. Each day, she worked harder to escape the feeling of being trapped by her children, but she no longer liked them. Laughter and games were replaced by a melancholy so heavy that even the neighbours kept away from the small family. Venus obsessively cleaned herself, the children and their home. She saved and moved to a larger apartment, got a better job as a nursery school assistant, enrolled the children in the same school. Parents and staff alike wondered at their neat, sad demeanour, but kept away.

On the girl's third birthday, Daktari appeared with gifts and a smile, as though he had just returned from a long business trip. He hugged the children, sat Boy on his knee and twinkled at Venus. Venus said nothing to him, neither welcoming or rejecting him, she did not see or hear him. When the children went to bed, she spoke for the first time.

'You want your son?'

He looked down at her crossed feet.

'I want us to be a family. I will marry you,' he said.

She got up, wiped the table, made some chai, placed a cup in front of him and sat down.

'How is this?' she asked. 'How do you do this thing? This hatred and fear of us and now this wanting us? We suffer too long alone for your silly games. We know how to live now. Leave us.' She walked away.

'I am so sorry. It took me time to understand that I loved you, all of you, that you are my destiny, my life, my purpose. I will be a good husband, a father to your daughter and our son. I have to go back home in a couple of months and I can't imagine life without you. Will you marry me? Share my life?'

Venus looked at him. He was thinner, less handsome, more ordinary. She took the steaming cup from his hand, poured the *chai* away and washed everything, carefully drying all the surfaces.

'You give me time to think. Now you go.'

Daktari returned every evening with more things, sweeter words, pleading smiles. After a month, he asked again. 'Venus, you have to make a decision, say yes or no tonight. I have no time left and I must make arrangements for me and my boy.'

She spun round and found him pressed against her.

'*Your* boy? The half-caste bastard you threw away a year ago? *Your* boy?'

Suddenly a large pot filled with greens and hot salt water crashed down on his head and a torrent of livid confusion poured out through the blows she aimed at his face, head, chest.

'Venus, oh Venus, I know, I know, there now, let it out, Daktari will make it better, Daktari will make it better.'

She wept into his chest, occasionally trying to pull away from his grasp. *This animal*, she thought, *this so-called man thinks a piece of paper can make us his? He is threatening to take the boy and offering marriage as compensation.* She rested against his chest, thought again: *I hate him enough to marry him, to make his life the living hell he has made mine.*

The decision made, she slumped against him and allowed herself to be carried to bed. Harris could not make love to her, he could not even fuck her, but he needed her, the children. He took her silence for consent and married her at the city hall two weeks before they flew to Birmingham.

In England, the family became inseparable. Venus couldn't speak the language well, barely understood the local accent and hated the cold. The food was alien and the people treated her and the children like strange animals. She could not bear to be away from her girl, but allowed Boy to be placed in a boarding school. He began speaking like Daktari and treated her like an unwelcome visitor.

She took a job at a kindergarten across the road from their home and obsessively cleaned her environment. She and the girl lived a secret life: playing, talking, sleeping, smiling. At midday and sometimes in the evenings when Daktari was late, they ate together, sharing the same bowl and utensils, drinking from the same cup, even though Daktari had bought six of everything. With the little girl, Venus lived the childhood she'd never had and was only disturbed when Boy joined them for the holidays.

During these times, Venus would scream and rage, throw things around the room and slap both her children. As her grasp of the language grew, she taunted Daktari with her memories of their meeting, the rape and his rejection of Boy. She demanded communication and could not hear. She lashed out with her tongue, her fists, and later with long, hate-filled silences. The girl took to surreptitiously watching her, gauging her mother's moods in order to decide whether to be jolly or invisible. Small scars appeared on the children's cheeks and tiny limbs. Daktari silently mended everyone and never spoke about the violence. He abhorred Venus's rage and feared her poisonous tongue, yet she was still devastatingly beautiful, still his Venus.

One day Harris told her he was looking for a job overseas.

'Back home?' she asked.

'No, not there. I was thinking I might go to Asia.'

She listened politely, didn't meet his eye and gave him a nod as if to say 'that is enough', before turning on her heel and hauling the vacuum cleaner out from under the stairs.

They said nothing more about his plans. Theirs had become a marriage of long silences. The words which neither of them verbalized weighed heavier than anything they said.

The silence occupied the dining table, then crept up the stairs into their bed so that they were both daily surprised by their disappointment. Eventually they slept in different rooms, lived separate lives.

A year later, he walked slowly down the stairs, straightening his tie. He was in no hurry. Breakfast was as usual. Coffee, toast, an egg boiled for three and a half minutes, butter and marmalade on the table. Tarnished silver salt and pepper cellars on the mat next to his setting, the *Birmingham Post* folded beside his side plate and his wife's hostile back standing over the kitchen sink. The girl cracked open her egg and began to chat brightly. He smiled, picked up the newspaper and concealed his face, allowing the paper to rustle against his shaking knees. He trembled with delighted anticipation. He made comments about his day, his step-daughter's new blazer, Venus's hair, the garden, with a sense of grace, generosity and new-found patience. He meant each word as a blessing, an act of compassion, and he imagined himself as a benevolent Jesus.

Venus had listened to him creeping down the stairs and her pretty nostrils curled up in disgust. She heard him struggle with the newspaper, each crunch and crush revealing that he was a small man with large pretensions. She listened to his comments with care, dissecting, analyzing and responding to them in her head; screaming, disagreeing with or rejecting each construction with wit, reason and formidable intellect.

A neat, clean crescent of shell lay beside the egg. Two slices of toast remained on the rack and a polite residue of cold coffee glazed in his cup.

'I'm leaving,' he said, sliding the paper an inch lower, careful not to reveal the broad sunlight of his smile. He peered at her. He no longer looked at her, just as she no longer saw him. Sometimes she heard him, but more often than not he was just a soft blur of shirt, tie or shoes. His packaging was all she cared about.

'Have a good day,' she said, looking up at the spot between his lowered eyes.

It irritated her that he had not moved. For a very short time, when she had first got used to his visits, his indecisiveness had seemed endearing, a form of consideration. *He was simply biding his time*, she thought, *so he could attack me, rape me, make the child with me then throw me away. Now look at him, all starched and buttoned up, pink and plump and spiritless*. She imagined a large wind-up key sticking out through the blue and white stripes of his shirt, just above his kidneys. Her lips twitched into a little smile. She saw herself winding and winding and winding until the spring went *clunk* and he broke like Boy's tin mice and rosy-cheeked drumming soldiers, which she killed by the hundred in her rages.

He glanced at his watch, pushed back his chair and hesitated, looking at his stepdaughter. 'You be good now, at this new school. Remember, you are a clever girl, cleverer than most of the others and don't let anyone hurt you with their words.' He stole a glance at his wife.

In the hall he opened his briefcase, stared into its contents for too long, pulled on his suit jacket, struggled into his coat and then rushed back into the kitchen.

'I . . .' The word hung in the air.

Swiftly he walked to the seated Venus, bent down and kissed her brow, nuzzled the girl's neck. 'Goodbye.' And he was gone.

She looked out through the kitchen window at the skies, at the patch of green garden and the shed.

The dull thud of the door closing behind him echoed in her head for years. He had not come home. During the first

215

agonized week she took to staring at the road through her pristine net curtains, listening for the click of keys in the front door, the slap-tap of mail on the floor. Sleep became heavy, pleasant, a relief from the waiting. She drank endless cups of coffee and decided not to call his surgery or his widowed mother. Discretion reigned supreme. After a few weeks, the girl stopped asking where Daddy was, and she didn't cry when Venus put her on a plane, back home to her grandmother. Venus moved Boy to a Christian Brothers boarding school in the north of England and sent him to camps for the holidays. She left her job and shut all the curtains in her house.

After six months she startled herself awake with a surge of adrenalin-fuelled grief. The house was a shambles, her matted hair stank and the debris of empty sherry bottles and coffee cups littered her thoughts. She washed, scrubbed and polished. It was only as she cleaned her body and home that she realized she had misplaced her wedding certificate.

When he returned – for he would return, she knew, like the last time, like he always did – she would tell him exactly what she thought about his behaviour and how he'd made her feel. She would punish him for the precise amount of time he'd been away by refusing to speak to him about anything other than bills, meals and memories. She would finally have the courage to tell him he didn't satisfy her as a husband and that she was considering looking elsewhere. He would have to put up with it and trust that she would be discreet. None of this would be news to him; God knew she had been as kind as she could, explaining what he did wrong and when. It was just too selfish of him to do this to her, to disappear without a word. Every day, at six forty-five a.m. precisely, she filled the kitchen with the reassuring smells of coffee, fresh toast and bacon, false domestic bliss. Sitting in her chair, opposite his place mat, she poured herself a dainty measure of bourbon and planned her search for the missing certificate. Each day she let the coffee grow cold, threw out tepid orange juice and slices of limp toast. Each morning she drank her bourbon from a crystal tumbler and began the search in a different room.

Banker's cheques in her name arrived regularly from around the globe. The mortgage on the house was suddenly paid off in a lump sum and the deeds were transferred to her name. There was no symmetry, no order in the size and shape of the envelopes, no apparent schedule to their arrival or rhythm in their contents. The sombre formality of Swiss stamps irritated her as much as the gay palms and shells on the Haitian ones. The foreignness of these places distressed her; she had a clear sense of a world that was contracting. The bourbon in the bottle diminished.

On one of these mornings, Mary, her grey-haired neighbour, pressed a photograph of Venus, Daktari and the children – taken in the front garden during their first sight of snow – into Venus's hand.

'This will remind you of who you are and where you came from,' the elderly woman whispered.

Venus stared at the faces: a young woman with over-large eyes and stern lines about the mouth looked back at her.

'That's you, bab. You beautiful child. I saw you trying so hard to be a good wife and mother. Perhaps you should have devoted yourself to being happy. If you carry on like this you will die young in a mental hospital. They say you drink. Well, love, I cared for you from the moment I met you. I saw who you really were before he left you. Did he abandon you before, bab? That man brought you from your country and shut you out of his life. Look at you now and look at that young woman when you feel the world closing in.'

Mary saw Venus smile and thought she had touched on

the truth, given comfort, witnessed another woman's story.

Venus tore away the other faces in the photograph, and kept the sliver of herself in her housecoat pocket. Thirty-one years old – angry, alone and too proud to seek compassion – she turned back to her quest for the marriage certificate. The bourbon tasted the same whether it was in a glass or straight out the bottle. She took to keeping several bottles around the house: stored in the cistern of the guest loo, warm between fluffy white towels, reclining among cotton pants and lacy brassieres, in the bedside cabinet behind her Bible. Nips and swigs relieved the disappointment of not finding the missing piece of paper. With each shifting of furniture and lifting of layers, the certificate grew more precious, meaningful and important. If only she could find it, everything would be all right. Nothing mattered but the daily search after breakfast. She would wake in the early hours, terrified and racked with horrifying cramps. Sometimes she would find herself on the bathroom floor, her housecoat wrapped in knots around her bloated body. Other times she came to crumpled against a broken piece of furniture in one of the unused rooms. Most often she gagged awake in his bedroom, covered in his clothes, sprawled in his brogues. She rarely slept in her own bed. In the hours before daybreak, she sipped bourbon and retched, sipped more until she stopped heaving and shaking. She would go to her bed and lie with the children's voices in her head until dawn, then she would scrub the smell of alcohol from her skin with salts and perfumes, put on a fresh housecoat and make breakfast for four while planning her search.

On a day like every other day, Venus opened her old suitcase, as she'd done hundreds of times in the past, and there at the bottom in a plain brown envelope lay the wedding certificate. The tiny scrap of her photographed face fell out

218

of her pocket on to the creased paper. The young woman in
the picture looked exactly like her, the same lines of bitter-
ness about the mouth, the same large troubled eyes, the same
mane of hair pulled harshly back. She carefully folded the
certificate, placed her photo on top and tucked them both
into the envelope. Slipping the small bundle into her pocket,
she walked back downstairs into the sparkly clean kitchen,
kicked off her slippers and glanced at the sealed envelope
that had arrived that morning. She picked it up to examine
the stamp. A family of four brown faces laughing idiotically
into the camera. She tore it, unopened, into tiny pieces and
puffing with rage, threw back her head to receive the
bourbon.

Today she would start her search in the shed.

A slow, secret smile spread across her face as she thought
of the wedding at the register office. How happy the children
had been, how hopeful Daktari had seemed, how vengeful
she had felt. She dragged two trunks of letters down the
garden path and locked herself in the cold shed, laughing
until she wept at the thought of Dr Harris, an elderly bloated
wreck, returning to search for her, the girl and his half-caste
bastard.

Mary called the police and fire brigade when she saw the
flames in the garden shed. They said Venus had scattered
old letters and papers around her, drenched the shed and
papers in petrol, then lit herself up.

Biographical Notes

Naylah Ahmed was born in Birmingham in 1976. She is a British Asian Muslim with Pakistani heritage. In 1998 her radio play, *Mrs Parker*, was one of four selected by BBC Radio 4, and was nominated by the Commission for Racial Equality for the Race in the Media Award for Radio Drama. Her second radio play, *The Happy Gathering*, will be aired on Radio 4 in 2001. She is presently co-writing a television drama series set in Bradford. Naylah is an official adviser for West Midlands Arts, and has been accepted on to the Writer's Attachment at the Birmingham Rep.

Kavita Bhanot, 23, was born in London. Her parents are from India. She came to Birmingham five years ago to study philosophy, and hasn't been able to get away. She is currently enjoying her MA in Post-Colonial Literature at Warwick University. This is her first published story.

Tonya Joy Bolton is a 23-year-old graduate of Jamaican descent. Born and bred in Birmingham, she has been writing all her life. Taking inspiration from black writers such as Alice Walker and Zora Neale Hurston, her poetry, essays and short stories examine race, gender and spirituality. Four of her poems have been published in *Griot* (Writers Without Borders, 2001). She is currently working on her MA and writing her first book of poetry.

Yvonne Brissett is a broadcast journalist at BBC Birmingham. Born in Gloucester to Jamaican parents, she moved to Birmingham to study Media at university. Her credits include BBC2's late-night entertainment series, *The A Force*; the award-winning BBC documentary series, *Windrush*, which celebrated fifty years of African-Caribbean presence in the UK; exclusive interviews with international R&B and hip-hop artistes such as Sean 'Puffy' Combs, Redman and Jodeci. On *Midlands Today* she continues to raise awareness of diverse communities within the West Midlands, and she is currently writing her first novel.

Maeve Clarke, 38, was shortlisted for the New Writers Award in 1996 and was a runner-up in the Stand International Fiction Competition 1999. She won third prize in the Alpha Omega Competition 2000 and her entry was published in an anthology of the same name. Maeve is a teacher of English as a Foreign Language and has taught in the UK, Spain and Italy, where she currently lives. She has written EFL educational material and her reader for students, *Give Us The Money!*, was published in 2001 by OUP. Maeve was born and raised in Birmingham. Her parents are Jamaican.

Rubina Din, 36, was born in Pakistan and has lived in Birmingham since she was a year old. Her parents are Pakistani Muslims. She began writing poetry, children's stories and prose fiction when she was twelve, and her non-fiction has been published in educational packages. She was invited on to a writing course run by East Midlands Arts because of a radio play she sent to the BBC, and she has attended screenwriting workshops at the Leicester Haymarket. Rubina was a finalist in the Focus on Talent 2 competition run by Black Coral.

Martin Glynn was born in Nottingham in 1957 to a Welsh mother and a Jamaican father. He now lives in Birmingham. He has worked with education and arts establishments in the USA, the Caribbean, Europe and the UK, developing literature initiatives, producing and directing performances,

221

and setting up residencies. He is a workshop facilitator and writes for theatre, radio drama, live performance and poetry collections, as well as pursuing an active career as a screen-play writer. He has published eleven books of poetry and his fiction has been widely anthologized in the UK.

Barrington Gordon is of African-Caribbean descent. He was born in Wolverhampton and now lives in Birmingham. He runs workshops in creative writing, drama and poetry. His story 'The Chair' was published in *Voice Memory Ashes: Lest We Forget*, edited by Jacob Ross and Joan Amin-Addo (Mango Publishing, 1999). He has completed one novel, *Men Cry Too*, is finishing his second and looks forward to develop-ing his career as a writer.

Kwa'mboka is half Kisii and half Kikuyu. An economist, curator, broadcaster, author and producer of performing arts, she is currently launching a web-based process 'Jua-Kali' (Fierce Sun) exploring the creativity of people of African heritage in and out of Europe. A nomad, she lives in a large tent pitched on the plains of the West Midlands.

Ava Ming was born in Birmingham in 1967. She is a classi-cally trained musician, experienced radio presenter – the *Ava Ming Show* ran on a local BBC radio station for six years – and has lectured in media studies. She is a regular con-tributor to newspapers and magazines and regularly writes short stories.

Ifemu Omari has written three stage plays, *Edge of the Circle* (1989), *Ruby* (1991) and *Dream Circus for Hire* (1993). She is a freelance lecturer in African and Caribbean literature and runs a company, WORD, which is involved in research work around women's history.

James Pogson, 32, was born in Birmingham. Both his parents are from St Kitts. A graduate in public administration and managerial studies, he has worked in the arts for more than a decade. He has written and produced ideas for radio and theatre, and he assisted in the co-ordination and facilitation of 'Carifesta VII – Caribbean Festival of Arts' held in August 2000 in St Kitts.

Leone Ross was born in Coventry in 1969. She grew up in Jamaica and returned to the UK in 1991. She is the author of two critically acclaimed novels, *All The Blood Is Red* (ARP, 1996) and *Orange Laughter* (Anchor Press/Farrar, Straus & Giroux, 2000). Her short fiction has been anthologized in the UK, USA and Canada, including the bestselling *Brown Sugar: A Collection of Black Erotica* (Dutton/Plume), *Dark Matter: A Century of Speculative Fiction from the African Diaspora* (Warner, 2000) and *Time Out London Short Stories, Volume 2* (Penguin, 2000). She lectures in short story writing at the City Literary Institute in London and won an Arts Council of England Writers Award in 2000. Her story 'Tasting Songs' was republished in the prestigious *Year's Best Fantasy and Horror* (St Martin's Press, USA, 2001). She was a journalist in another life.

Norman Samuda-Smith, 42, was born in Birmingham. His parents came from Jamaica to the UK in the 1950s. He currently works at the University of Central England, Birmingham, in the art and design library. Norman has had short stories published by community organizations, as well as acting in and writing plays in the 1980s for a theatre company, Ebony Arts, of which he was a founder member. His novel, *Bad Friday*, was first published in 1982 by Trinity Arts, Birmingham, was shortlisted for the Young Observer Fiction

Prize in that year, and was republished by New Beacon Books in 1985.

Amina Shelly, 24, was born in Sylhet, Bangladesh, into a Muslim family. She has lived in the UK since 1989. She is a poet, short story writer and an artistic photographer. Her work involves her girlhood, religion, tradition, culture and social struggles starting from her birthplace to the far west. Currently translating Bengali fiction into English and vice versa, she is an ex-sales administrator who works for a living in her spare time.

Pavan Deep Singh was born and raised in Smethwick in the West Midlands. He graduated from the University of Wolverhampton with a degree in media, art and design. He is a community development officer, working with local people at grassroots level. He draws his inspiration from Punjabi folk legends and experiences of growing up in a culturally diverse community. His story 'Freshies With Attitude' was published in *England Calling* (Weidenfeld & Nicolson, 2001).

Beverley Wood was born and raised in Birmingham. Her parents are from Jamaica. After graduating, Beverley trained as a journalist and worked as a freelance writer before joining the BBC as a television producer, scriptwriter and film maker. She is chair of West Midlands Disability Arts Forum and has edited their publication *d'art*. She is currently working as a diversity co-ordinator in the Black Country.